A NIGHT
OF NO RETURN

A NIGHT OF NO RETURN

BY

SARAH MORGAN

First published in Great Britain 2012
by Mills & Boon, an imprint of Harlequin (UK) Limited.
Large Print edition 2013
Harlequin (UK) Limited, Eton House,
18-24 Paradise Road, Richmond, Surrey TW9 1SR

© Sarah Morgan 2012

ISBN: 978 0 263 23167 0

Printed and bound in Great Britain
by CPI Antony Rowe, Chippenham, Wiltshire

CHAPTER ONE

IT WAS the one night of the year he dreaded more than any other.

In the beginning he'd tried everything in a bid to escape it—wild parties, women, work—but he'd discovered that it didn't matter what he was doing or who he was doing it with, the pain remained the same. He chose to live his life in the present, but the past was part of him and he carried it everywhere. It was a memory that wouldn't fade. A scar that wouldn't heal. A pain that went bone-deep. There *was* no escape, which was why his favoured way of spending this particular night was to find somewhere he could be alone and get very, very drunk.

He'd driven the two hours from his office in London to the property he was restoring in rural Oxfordshire simply for the privilege of being alone. For once his phone was switched off, and it was staying that way.

Snow swirled in a crazy dance in front of the windscreen and visibility was down to almost zero. Huge white drifts were piled high at the side of the road, a trap for the nervous, inexperienced driver.

Lucas Jackson was neither nervous nor inexperienced and his mood was blacker than the weather.

The howl of the wind sounded like a child screaming and he clenched his jaw and tried to blot out the noise.

Never had the first glimpse of stone lions guarding the entrance to his estate been so welcome. Despite the conditions he barely slowed his pace, accelerating along the long drive that wound through acres of parkland towards the main house.

He drove past the lake, now frozen into a skating rink for the ducks, over the bridge that crossed the river and heralded the final approach to Chigworth Castle.

He waited to feel the rush of satisfaction that should have come from owning this, but as always there was nothing. It shouldn't have surprised him, he'd long since accepted that he wasn't able to feel in the way that other people did. He'd switched that part of himself off and he hadn't been able to switch it on again.

What he did experience as he looked at the magnificent building was a detached appreciation for something that satisfied both the mathematician in him and the architect. The dimensions and structure were perfect. A gatehouse presided over the entrance, its carved stonework creating a first impression that was both imposing and aesthetically pleasing. And then there was the castle itself, with its buff stonework and battlements that attracted the interest of historians from around the world. The knowledge that he was preserving history gave him a degree of professional pride, but as for the rest of it—the personal, emotional side—he felt nothing.

Whoever said that revenge was a dish best eaten cold had been wrong.

He'd sampled it and found it tasteless.

And tonight Lucas wasn't even interested in the historical significance of the house, just its isolation. It was miles from the nearest hint of civilisation and that suited him just fine. The last thing he wanted tonight was human contact.

Lights burned in a few of the upstairs windows and he frowned because he'd specifically instructed the staff to take the night off. He was in no mood for company of any description.

He drove over the bridge that spanned the moat, under the arch that guarded the entrance and skidded the last few metres into the courtyard, his tyres sending snow spinning into the air.

It occurred to him that if he hadn't left the office when he had, he might not have made it. He had staff capable of clearing the roads in the estate, but the approach to the house consisted of a network of winding country lanes that were a low priority for the authorities responsible for their upkeep. Briefly he thought of Emma, his loyal PA, who had stayed late at the office yet again in order to help him prepare for his coming trip to Zubran, an oil-rich state on the Persian Gulf. It was a good job she lived in London and wouldn't have far to travel home.

Abandoning the car to the weather, he strode

across the snowy carpet and let himself in to the darkness of the entrance hall.

No housekeeper to greet him tonight. No staff. No one. Just him.

'Surprise!!' A chorus of voices erupted from around him and lights blazed.

Temporarily blinded, Lucas froze, shock holding him immobile on his own doorstep.

'Happy birthday to me!' Tara walked forward, a sway in her hips and a sly smile on her beautiful face as she hooked a finger inside his coat and lifted her scarlet painted mouth to his. 'I know you promised to give me my present next week, but I can't wait that long. I want it *now*.'

Lucas stared down into those famous blue eyes and still felt nothing.

Slowly, deliberately, he detached her hand from the front of his coat. 'What the hell,' he asked quietly, 'are you doing here?'

'Celebrating my birthday.' Clearly less than delighted with his chilly response, she produced her trademark pout. 'You refused to come to my party so I decided to bring the party to you. Your housekeeper let us in. Why haven't you ever invited me here before? I *love* this place. It's like a film set.'

Lucas lifted his gaze. He saw now that the grand hall with its magnificent paintings and tapestries had been decorated with streamers and balloons. Gaudily wrapped presents were stacked next to a large iced birthday cake. Open bottles of champagne stood on an antique table, mocking his black mood.

Never in his life had he felt less like celebrating.

His first thought was that he was going to fire his housekeeper, but then he remembered just how persuasive Tara could be when she wanted something. She was a master at manipulating emotions and he knew it frustrated her that she'd never succeeded in manipulating his.

'Tonight is not a good night for me. I told you that.' His voice sounded robotic but Tara simply shrugged dismissively.

'Well, whatever it is that is making you so moody, you need to snap out of it, Lucas. You'll forget about it once you've had a drink. We'll dance for a bit and then go upstairs and—'

'Get out.' His thickened command was greeted

with appalled silence. Her friends—people he didn't know and had no desire to know—murmured their shock.

The only person who seemed unaffected by his response was Tara herself whose ego was the least fragile thing about her. 'Don't be ridiculous, Lucas. You don't mean that. It's a surprise party.'

But the surprise, apparently, was his. *Only Tara could hold a surprise party for her own birthday.* 'Get out and take your friends with you.'

Her eyes hardened. 'We all came by coach and it isn't coming back until one o'clock.'

'When did you last look outside? Nothing is going to be moving on these roads by one o'clock. That coach had better be here in the next ten minutes or you'll be snowed in. And trust me, you do *not* want that.' Perhaps it was his tone, perhaps it was the fact that he looked dangerous—and he knew that he must look dangerous because he *felt* dangerous—but his words finally sank home.

Tara's beautiful face, that same face that had graced so many magazine covers, turned scarlet with humiliation and anger. Those cat-like eyes flashed into his, but what she saw there must have scared her because the colour fled from her cheeks and left her flawless skin as pale as the winter snow blanketing the ground outside.

'Fine.' Her lips barely moved. 'We'll take our party elsewhere and leave you alone with your horrid temper for company. Now I know why your relationships don't last. Money, brains and skill in bed can't make up for the fact that you don't have a heart, Lucas Jackson.'

He could have told her the truth. He could have told her that his heart, once intact and fully functioning, had been damaged beyond repair. He could have told her that the phrase 'time heals' was false and that he was living proof that damage could be permanent. He could have described the relief that came from knowing he might never be healed because a heart already damaged could never be damaged again.

There was something beating in his chest, that was true, but it did nothing more than pump blood around his body, enabling him to get out of bed in the morning and go to work every day.

He could have told Tara all of that but she

would have gained as little satisfaction in the listening as he would in the telling, so he simply strode past her towards the famous oak staircase that rose majestically from the centre of the hall.

Tonight the proportions and design gave him no satisfaction. The staircase was merely a means to escape from the people who had invaded his sanctuary.

Without waiting for them to leave, he took the stairs two at a time and strode towards his bedroom in the tower that overlooked the moat.

He didn't care that he'd shocked them.

He didn't care that he'd ended yet another relationship.

All he cared about was getting through this one night.

He was a cold-hearted, driven workaholic.

Her normal patience nowhere to be found, Emma struggled to keep the car on the road. It was Friday night and she should have been at home relaxing with Jamie. Instead, she was chasing her boss round the English countryside. After the week she'd had it was the last thing she needed. She had a *life*, for goodness' sake.

Or rather, she would have liked to have a life. Unfortunately for her, she worked for a man for whom the concept of a life outside work didn't exist.

Lucas Jackson didn't have any emotional attachments and clearly didn't think his staff should have them either. He wasn't interested in her as a person, just in her contribution to his company. And there would have been no point in explaining her feelings because, as far as she could tell, he didn't have feelings. His life was so far removed from hers that sometimes when she drove into her space in the car park beneath the iconic glass building that housed the world-renowned architectural firm of Jackson and Partners, she felt as if she'd arrived on another planet. Even the building itself was futuristic—a tribute to cutting-edge design and energy efficiency, designed to maximise daylight and natural ventilation, a bold statement that represented the creative vision and genius of just one man. Lucas Jackson.

But creative vision and genius required focus and single-minded determination and that combination together created a driven, difficult human being. More machine than human, she thought moodily as she peered through the thick falling snow in an attempt to not end her days in a ditch.

When she'd started working for him two years previously she hadn't minded that their conversation was never personal. She didn't want or expect it when she was at work, so that suited her well. The one thing she would never, *ever* do was fall in love with her boss. But she'd fallen in love with her job. The work was interesting, stimulating and in every way that mattered Lucas was an excellent employer, despite the fact that his reputation had unnerved her to the point where she almost hadn't applied for the role. She'd found him to be professional, bright and a generous payer and it excited her to be involved with a company responsible for the design of some of the most famous buildings of recent times. He was undoubtedly a genius. Those were his positive points.

The negatives were that he was focused on work to the exclusion of everything else.

Take this week. Preparations for the official opening of the Zubran Ferrara Resort, an innovative eco hotel nestling on the edge of the warm waters of the Persian Gulf, had driven her workload from crazy to manic. Fuelled by caffeine, she'd stayed until the early hours every night in an attempt to complete essential work. Not once had she complained or commented on the fact that, generally, she expected to be fast asleep by two a.m. and preferably not at her desk.

The one thing that had kept her going had been the thought of Friday. The start of her holiday. Two whole weeks that she took off every year over the festive season. She'd visualised that time in the way a marathon runner might imagine the finish line. It had been the shining light at the end of a tunnel of exhaustion.

And then the snow had started falling. And falling. All week it had been snowing steadily until by Friday London was half empty.

All day Emma had been eyeing the weather out of the window. She'd seen staff from other office buildings leaving early, slithering and sliding their way through the snow to be sure of making it home. As Lucas's PA she had the authority to extend that privilege to other more junior staff and she had, until the only two people remaining in the building had been herself and her ruthlessly focused boss.

Lucas hadn't appeared to notice the snow-storm transforming the world into a death zone. When she'd mentioned it, he hadn't responded. That would have been bad enough and suffi-cient to have her cursing him for her entire jour-ney home but just as she'd been about to turn out the lights, the last to leave as usual, she'd noticed the file sitting on his desk. It was the file she'd put together for his trip to Zubran and it included papers that needed his signature. A helicopter would be picking him up from his country house. He wouldn't be coming back to the office.

At first she didn't believe he could have for-gotten it. Lucas never forgot anything. He was the most efficient person she'd ever worked for. And once she'd come to terms with the fact that for some reason his usual efficiency had chosen a frozen Friday night to desert him, she'd faced a dilemma.

She'd tried calling him, hoping to catch him while he was still in London, but his phone con-tinually switched to voicemail, presumably because he was already talking to someone else. Lucas spent his life talking on the phone.

She could have arranged a courier, but the file contained confidential and sensitive information and she didn't trust it with anyone but herself. Did that make her obsessive? Possibly. But if it were to be mislaid she would be out of a job and she wasn't about to take that risk.

Which was why she was now, late on a miserable Friday night when no one else with any sense would be on the roads, heading west out of London towards his rural country house.

Emma squinted through the white haze. She didn't mind hard work. Her only rule was that she didn't work at weekends. And for some reason—maybe her references, maybe her calm demeanour, or just the fact that he'd lost six PAs in as many months—Lucas Jackson had accepted that one caveat, although he had once made a caustic comment about her 'wild social life'.

If he'd taken the trouble to find out about her, he would have known that there wasn't room for 'wild' in her life. He would know that the nearest she'd got to a party was through the pages of the celebrity magazines her sister occasionally bought. He would have known that after working a punishing week at Jackson and Partners her idea of a perfect weekend was just sleeping late and spending time with Jamie. Lucas would have known all that, but he didn't because he'd never asked.

She glanced briefly at the offending file on the passenger seat next to her, as if by simply glaring at it she might somehow manage to teleport the contents to its owner.

Unfortunately there was no chance of that. Her only choice was to take it to him. Never let it be said that she didn't do her job properly.

This launch was the most talked about event for a decade and the party itself would be a glittering gathering of everyone important. Emma had felt a wistful pang as she'd liaised with Avery Scott, the dynamic owner of Dance and Dine, the company in charge of organising the launch event. From her conversations with Avery, she knew that the international celebrity guest list would be indulging in vintage champagne in the glamour of a marquee designed as a Bedouin tent. Then they would enjoy a traditional Zubrani banquet under the stars and have the opportunity to explore the specially constructed 'souk', tempting the guests with various local delicacies and entertainment. To showcase the best of Zubran as a holiday destination there would be belly dancers, fortune tellers, falconry and the evening would conclude with what promised to be the most spectacular firework display ever witnessed.

This was probably how Cinderella had felt when she'd learned she would not be going to the ball, Emma thought gloomily.

Shivering in the freezing air that her inadequate heater didn't manage to warm, she sank deeper inside her coat and allowed herself a brief fantasy involving sunshine and palm trees. Just for a moment she felt envious. Right now this minute, the women on the guest list were probably deciding what to wear and packing for a break in the sun where all they were expected to do was look glamorous.

Emma pushed her hair away from her face with her gloved hand. She didn't need to look in the mirror to know she didn't look glamorous. She looked wrecked.

Forget celebrity parties. She'd be thrilled just

to be able to get to bed before midnight. And if the weather carried on like this, she and Jamie would be spending their precious holiday trapped indoors.

She was struggling to keep the car on the icy road when her phone rang.

She thought it might be Lucas finally returning one of her many frantic messages, but it wasn't. It was Jamie.

Of course it was Jamie. He'd expected her over an hour ago.

'Where are you, Emma?' His concern was audible in his voice and she suddenly felt horribly disloyal for wishing she could have gone to Zubran and partied under the stars.

Not daring to drive and talk with the road conditions so bad, she pulled over, squashing down the guilt. 'I had to work late. I'm so sorry. I left you a message.'

'When will you be home?'

'Soon. I hope.' She stared doubtfully at the falling snow. 'But it might take me a while because the roads are terrible. Don't wait up.'

He didn't say anything and she knew he was upset with her.

His silence made her guilt worse. While he'd been worrying, she'd been imagining the perfect dress to wear to the party of the decade. 'We have the whole weekend to be together and next week,' she reasoned. When there was still no answer, she gave a sigh. 'Jamie, don't be upset. I have to work tonight. It's never happened before. You know I normally keep the weekends free but this is an emergency. Lucas left some really important papers and I have to take them to him.'

It was a difficult conversation and by the time she hung up she was cursing Lucas Jackson with words she never normally allowed herself to use. Why couldn't he have remembered the stupid file? Or why couldn't he at least get off the phone and pick up her calls? At least then she could have met him halfway or something.

Knowing that the only thing that was going to make her feel better was getting the job done and going home, she eased the car back onto the road. Her eyes felt gritty and her head throbbed. She couldn't wait to just crawl into bed and sleep and sleep.

She'd make it up to Jamie. They had two weeks

together—the whole of the Christmas holidays. Two whole weeks while her high-flying boss was in Zubran, locked in business meetings with the Sultan and partying the night away under the stars. And she wasn't jealous. Absolutely not.

Visibility was down to virtually zero. She lost her way twice in the maze of country lanes that all looked the same and defeated her satnav. The only car on the road, she crawled her way along a snowy lane and finally found herself at the entrance to Chigworth Castle.

Two huge stone lions snarled down at her from either side of the open gates and she glared back at them, thinking that the house was about as friendly and welcoming as the man who owned it.

By the time she'd slithered and skidded her way down a drive that seemed as long as the road to London, the throb in her head was worse and she'd convinced herself she'd taken a wrong turn. This couldn't possibly be right. It was leading nowhere.

Where on earth was the actual house? Did one person really need this much land?

Her headlights picked out a wood and a lake

and she drove over a bridge, tyres skidding, turned a corner and saw it. Floodlit with warm beams of light that illuminated honey-coloured stone and tall, beautiful windows, a small castle stood as it had no doubt stood for centuries, surrounded by a moat.

'Battlements,' Emma breathed, enchanted. 'It even has battlements.'

Snow clung to those battlements and smoke twirled from a chimney into the cold air. Lights shone from a tower in one corner of the building and her mouth literally fell open because she'd had no idea that he owned something like this. He was all about modern, cutting-edge design and yet this—this imposing, beautiful building was part of history.

It really was a castle. A small, but perfectly formed castle.

Small? Emma gave a choked laugh. Small was her rented room in one of the less salubrious areas of London. She had a single window that overlooked a train line and was woken every morning at five a.m. by the aeroplanes landing at Heathrow Airport. Idyllic living it was not. This, however, was. So much space, she thought enviously. Acres of gardens, now cloaked in white but easy enough to imagine them in the spring— carpets of bluebells stretching endlessly into the wood where currently there was nothing but layers of soft, unmarked snow.

It was truly beautiful.

For a moment her eyes stung and she wondered how a house could possibly make her want to cry.

It wasn't that perfect, was it?

For a start it was isolated. Realising just how isolated, Emma gave a shiver as she coaxed her little car forward over the bridge that spanned the moat. She might have been the only person on the planet.

And then through the archway she saw the sleek, familiar lines of Lucas's car, already almost obscured by the falling snow. So he'd made it, but he still wasn't answering his phone.

Resolving to buy him a phone that only she used and relieved to still be in one piece, she sat for a moment, waiting for her heart rate to slow down. When she was sufficiently recovered, she reached for the offending file.

Two minutes, Emma promised herself as she

switched off the engine and stepped carefully out of the car. This was going to take her two minutes. As soon as she'd handed over the file, she'd get back on the road.

The moment her feet touched the ground, she slipped. Crashing down awkwardly in her attempt to protect the file, she bumped her elbow and her head. For a moment she lay there, winded, and then she rolled onto her knees and struggled back to her feet. Bruised, damp and angry, she picked her way gingerly towards the door, the snow seeping through her shoes.

She stabbed the bell with her finger and held it there, taking small comfort from that minor rebellion. There was no answer.

Snow trickled down from her hair to her neck and from there inside her shirt.

Emma shivered and rang the bell again, surprised that someone hadn't immediately opened the door. She'd assumed the place would be crawling with staff and Lucas was notoriously intolerant of inefficiency of any kind.

Someone, she thought, was going to be in trouble.

Having rung the bell for a third time and still

received no response, she tried the door with no expectation that it would open.

When it did, she hesitated on the threshold. Walking into someone else's home uninvited wasn't a habit of hers, but she had a file he needed and she wasn't about to drive it all the way back to the office.

'Hello?' Cautiously, she peeped her head in through the door, bracing herself to set off an alarm. But there was no sound and she opened the door further. She saw dark wood panelling, tapestries, huge oil paintings and a sweeping staircase so romantic that it made a girl long for Rhett Butler to stride into the house and sweep her off her feet. When there was still no sign of life, she stepped inside.

'Hello?' She closed the door to keep the heat in—*how much did it cost to heat somewhere like this?*—and then noticed the open champagne bottles, the balloons and the streamers. And a cake. Something about the cake didn't quite seem right, but she couldn't work out what it was. Clearly a party was going on somewhere, except there was no sign of any guests, just an overpowering silence that was almost creepy.

She half expected someone to jump out from behind the heavy velvet curtains and shout *boo*!

An uneasy feeling crept down her spine. For goodness' sake, it was just a house! A big house, admittedly, but there was nothing threatening about a house. And she wasn't alone. She couldn't possibly be alone. Lucas had to be here somewhere and a whole load of other people judging from the number of champagne bottles.

Hoping that an enormous guard dog wasn't about to bound out and close its jaws on a sensitive part of her anatomy, Emma walked over to a large oak door and pushed it open. It was a library, the walls lined with tall bookshelves stacked with books bound in various faded shades of old leather.

'Lucas?' She tentatively explored all the obvious rooms on the ground floor and then walked up the staircase. This was ridiculous. She couldn't search the whole house. Remembering the light she'd seen shining from the tower, she decided to just try there.

Hazarding a guess as to the correct direction, she turned right and walked along a carpeted corridor until she reached a heavy oak door.

She tapped once and opened it. 'Lucas?' A spiral staircase rose in front of her and she walked up it and found herself in a large circular room with windows on all sides. Logs blazed in a huge fireplace and out of the corner of her eye she caught sight of a huge four-poster bed draped in moss-green velvet, but her attention was on the low leather sofa because there, sprawled with his feet up on the arm and a bottle of champagne in his hand, was her boss.

'Lucas?'

'I thought I told you to get out.' His savage tone made her gasp and she took a step backwards and almost tumbled down the stairs. Not once in the years she'd worked for him had he spoken to her like that.

One glance told her that he was rip-roaring drunk and she so rarely saw him out of control that her initial reaction was one of surprise. The fact that he didn't make a habit of it did nothing to soothe her bruised feelings.

While her Friday night had been well and truly ruined, he'd been enjoying himself. He'd switched his phone off not because he was busy with an important business call, but because he

was busy getting drunk. She'd risked her neck
driving around the English countryside in a
snowstorm, while all the time Lucas was warm
and snug in front of a roaring log fire drinking
champagne. Not only that, he had the gall to tell
her to get out.

Emma's temper, usually slow to burn, began
to glow hot.

She was about to slap the file down on the
table and leave him to his solitary party when
she suddenly realised that what he'd actually
said wasn't *get out* but 'I thought I told you to
get out.'

She frowned.

He certainly hadn't already told her to get out.
Which could only mean that he thought she was
someone else.

She remembered the balloons and the streamers. The abandoned champagne bottles. The
cake.

'Lucas!' She spoke more clearly this time. 'It's
me. Emma.'

For a moment she thought he hadn't heard her,
and then his eyes opened.

Across the shadowy room she saw the lethal

glitter that told her everything she needed to know about his mood. She was nowhere near him and yet it was as if he'd reached out and touched her. Her body warmed. She shifted uncomfortably. She'd never seen him like this before. The man she knew was always sleek and groomed. His suits were handmade in Italy, his shirts custom-made. He was a man who expected the best in everything. A sophisticated connoisseur of all things beautiful.

But tonight he looked dangerous in every way. In mood. In looks. His shirt was open at the neck, exposing a cluster of dark hair and a hint of powerful chest. Shadowy stubble darkened his strong jaw and, most disturbingly of all, she had the feeling that he was balancing on the very edge of control.

Sensing it, Emma reacted the way she would have reacted had she suddenly been confronted by a snarling Rottweiler intent on ripping her throat out. She froze and tried to project calm. 'It's just me,' she said soothingly, 'only you seemed to think I was someone else, so I thought I ought to just clarify that…er…it's me.'

The silence stretched for such an agonizing

length of time that she'd started to think that he wasn't going to answer when suddenly he stirred.

'Emma?' His voice was soft and deadly and did nothing to reassure her.

She discovered that her hands were shaking and that irritated her. This was Lucas, for goodness' sake. She'd worked with him almost every day for two years. He was tough, but he wasn't threatening. Not exactly kind, but not cruel either. 'I've been calling you for hours. Why didn't you pick up the phone?'

'Who the hell let you in?'

'No one. I rang the bell and no one answered so I—' She broke off and he raised an eyebrow.

'So you thought you'd just walk into my house? Tell me, Little Red Riding Hood, do you make a habit of walking through the forest when the wolf is loose?' Fierce blue eyes met hers and Emma felt as if she were being suffocated.

She lifted her hand and loosened the scarf around her neck. Maybe it was his tone. Maybe it was the look in his eyes, but suddenly her heart was pounding. 'I rang the bell. You didn't answer.'

'But you walked in anyway.' Those softly spoken words were a million times more disturbing than the hard tone he'd used to order her out.

She tried to rally herself. 'If you had answered your phone I wouldn't have had to walk in.'

'My phone is switched off. And I didn't answer the door because I wasn't looking for company.'

Something snapped inside her. 'You think I drove for over two hours in lethal conditions for the pleasure of your company? After the week we've had, when I've had your "company" for an average of fifteen hours a day? I don't think so.' The injustice of it stoked her temper. 'I drove here, at much personal inconvenience, I might add, to give you a file. The file that you forgot to pick up. The file you need tomorrow.'

'Tomorrow?' The way he said it made it sound as if that day were a lifetime away. A point somewhere in the future that might never come.

'Yes, tomorrow.' She looked at him in exasperation. Was he really that drunk? 'Zubran? The launch party? Your papers for the Ferrara meeting? Is any of this ringing any bells with you?' She'd been clutching the file to her chest like a shield but now she thrust it towards him and then decided that on second thoughts she didn't want him to move from the sofa, so instead she dropped it on the nearest table. 'There. My job is done. You can thank me when you're sober.'

Slowly, he put the champagne down on the floor. 'You drove out here to give me the file?'

'Yes, I did.' And suddenly she felt like a crazy person for doing that. 'You need it. I didn't want to trust it to a courier.'

'You could have given it to Jim.'

Jim was his driver. 'Jim has flown to Dublin for a long weekend.' Why hadn't he remembered that? *What was the matter with him?*

'So you chose to bring it in person.' His eyes glinted in the firelight and his gaze slowly travelled from her head to her toes as if he was seeing her properly for the first time.

'Yes, I brought it to you in person,' she snapped, hating herself for caring that she wasn't looking her best. It wasn't that she had any expectations of coming close to meeting his standards of visual perfection, but it would have boosted her confidence and made her feel businesslike. As it was, it was hard to feel businesslike with mud and snow streaked down her coat. 'Frankly

I'm starting to wish I hadn't bothered, since the gesture clearly isn't appreciated.'

'Your head is bleeding. And your hair is wet. What happened to you?'

There was blood? Emma touched her head with her fingers and felt the bruise. Oh God, there *was* blood. How embarrassing. She rummaged in her bag for a tissue and pressed it against her head. 'I slipped walking from the car. It's fine.' Suddenly she was horribly aware that it was just the two of them in this enormous house. It didn't matter that she was often alone with him in the office. This felt different. 'I'm going now and I'll leave you to your party.' She thought again about the balloons and the cake and wondered where everyone else was. In a different part of the house?

'Ah yes, my party.' He gave a humourless laugh and his head dropped back against the sofa. 'Go, Emma. Someone like you shouldn't be here.'

She'd been about to retreat but his words stopped her. Offended, she tapped her foot on the floor. 'By "someone like me" I assume you mean someone who doesn't move in your lofty social circle.'

'I didn't mean that, but it doesn't matter.'

Stung, she stood still for a moment. 'Actually it does matter. I've just risked my neck and upset someone I love to bring you a file you don't even remember needing. A "thank you" would be nice. Manners are a good thing to have.'

'But I'm not nice. And I'm certainly not good.' His bitter tone shocked her. Her anger fizzled out.

'Lucas—'

'Get out, Emma.' This time he used her name so that there could be no mistake about whom he was addressing. 'Get out and close the damn door behind you.'

CHAPTER TWO

OF ALL the ungrateful, rude, pig-headed... Emma stomped down the stairs, along the landing and down the main staircase, swept forward by rolling waves of righteous anger.

Get out, Emma.

Get out, Emma.

Those words rang in her ears and she set her teeth and walked faster.

Well, she was getting out. She couldn't get out fast enough.

She consoled herself that at least her conscience was clear. She'd done her job. She'd given him the file. No one could accuse her of behaving unprofessionally. Now she could relax and enjoy the holidays with Jamie without suffering a nagging worry that she should have done more. Lucas had made it clear that his personal life was his own business and that was just fine with her.

Her footsteps echoed in the magnificent hall-way as she stormed towards the door. There was still no sign of anyone else and she wondered why a party would have finished so early.

I told you to get out!

His words played over and over again in her head. Who had he told to get out?

Telling herself that his manners were none of her business, she pulled open the door. The cold slammed into her and she gasped and hud-dled into her damp coat. Even in the compara-tively short time she'd been inside, the weather had turned seriously ugly. The snow was falling twice as heavily. Already her footprints were covered and her car was an amorphous white blob.

Her head still aching from her last unsched-uled contact with the ground, Emma picked her way gingerly to her car and knocked the worst of the snow off the windscreen with her glove. If that much snow had fallen since she'd been in the house then the bridge she'd crossed to get here would pretty soon be impassable. Her little car wouldn't be able to cope with the combina-tion of the snow and the gradient.

With that thought in her head, she was about to slide into the driver's seat and start the engine when something about the smooth, untouched mound of snow on the roof made her think of the cake. And thinking of the cake made her realise what it was that had been bothering her. The cake was untouched. Whole. It hadn't been cut. Not a single slice had been taken from it.

Emma stood for a moment, one leg in the car, the other on the snowy ground, wondering about that. The celebration, whatever it was, had obviously stopped before they'd reached the part with the cake.

I told you to get out.

She tightened her lips and slid into the car. It wasn't any of her business. Wrapping her freezing fingers around the key, she started the engine. Maybe he didn't like cake. Maybe he didn't have a sweet tooth. Maybe—

'Drat and bother.' Switching off the engine, she thumped her head back against the seat. He'd told her to get out. If she had any sense she'd do just that.

Slowly she turned her head and looked back at the house.

He'd said he wanted to be alone so that was exactly what she should do. Leave him alone.

She tightened her hands on the wheel.

Whatever was wrong with Lucas Jackson wasn't any of her business.

Lucas stared blindly into the dying flames of the fire. He was drunk, but nowhere near as drunk as he wanted to be. The pain was as acute as ever. It was like lying down on the business end of a saw, feeling the teeth digging into every single part of him. Nothing he did could ease it.

Standing up, he walked to the basket of logs by the fire and pulled one out.

'You shouldn't be doing that. You'll burn the whole place down if you're not careful.' A female voice came from the doorway and he turned, wondering if he were hallucinating.

Emma stood there. Her cheeks were pink from the cold, snowflakes sparkled and clung to her dark hair and her eyes were frosty. He wasn't sure if he was seeing anger or defiance but he knew he was looking at trouble and he straightened slowly.

'I thought I told you—'

'—to get out. Yes, you did, which was very rude of you actually.' Her tone was brisk. 'For future reference, you *deserve* to be left on your own if that is the way you speak to people.' She lifted her hand and unwound her scarf from around her neck, sending snow fluttering onto the thick rug that covered the floor of the turret bedroom.

'That's what I want,' Lucas said slowly. 'I *want* to be left on my own.' He enunciated every syllable, aware that his emotions were dangerously close to the surface. 'I thought I'd made that clear.'

'You did.'

'So what are you doing here?'

'Sticking my nose into your business.' She tugged off a soaking-wet glove. 'For selfish reasons. I'm about to go on holiday. I don't want to spend that time worrying that you've fallen into the fire in a drunken stupor.'

'Why would that bother you?'

'If something happens to you I'd have to look for a new job and it's rubbish out there right now.'

'You don't have to worry.' Lucas tightened

his hand on the log and felt the rough bark cut into his palm. 'I'm not that drunk, although I'm working on it.'

'Which is why I can't leave. When you stop "working on it" I'll be able to go.' The other glove went the same way as the first, the soaked fabric clinging to her skin. 'In the meantime, I don't want your death on my conscience.'

'I am not about to die.' He heard the anger in his voice and wondered why she couldn't hear it too. 'You can leave with a clear conscience. If you have any sense you'll do it. Right now.'

'I'm not leaving until you've told me why there seems to have been a party downstairs but you're on your own in the house.'

'Despite all my best attempts, I am *not* alone. *You're* here. And frankly I don't understand why. I've been rude to you. If you have any self-respect you should probably punch me and resign on the spot.'

'That only happens in the movies. In real life no one can afford to resign on the spot and only someone with your wealth would even suggest such a rash course of action.' Shivering, she unbuttoned her soaking coat and stepped closer to the fire. 'And self-respect means different things to different people. Dramatic overreaction isn't really my style, but if I walked away from someone in trouble *then* I'd lose all self-respect.'

'Emma—'

'And although it's true that you do lack empathy and certain human characteristics like a conscience, you are actually a reasonable person to work for most of the time so resigning would be a pretty stupid thing to do. Truth is, I love my job. And as for punching you—I've never punched anyone or anything in my life, although I did come close in the supermarket last week but that's another story. And anyway, my hands are so cold from scraping snow from the car I don't think I can even form a fist.' She flexed her fingers experimentally while Lucas watched with mounting exasperation.

Apparently wealth and success couldn't buy a man time alone when he wanted it.

'You love your job? In that case I am giving you a direct order,' he said in a thickened tone. 'Leave now or I *will* fire you.'

'You can't fire me. Not only would that be unfair dismissal but, technically, I'm now on my own time. Weekend time. How I spend it is my decision and no one else's.'

'Weekend time that previously you've always refused to work. Why pick this particular moment to break your unbreakable rule?' Anger exploded. 'Surely there is somewhere you need to be? What about this exciting life you live at weekends?' He remembered the one occasion, right at the beginning of her employment when she'd taken a personal call within his hearing. 'Why aren't you rushing home to Jamie?'

Her eyebrows rose in surprise. 'You know about Jamie?'

'Nothing to do with empathy or conscience.' Lucas was quick to dispel that possible thought before it even formed. 'I just have a good memory.'

'I didn't realise you knew about Jamie. And I will be going home, once I've assured myself you're OK.'

'I'm OK. You can see I'm OK.'

'There's no need to speak through your teeth and actually I don't see someone who is OK. I see a man who is drunk. On his own. A man who doesn't usually drink. Something seriously weird is going on.' She tapped her foot on the floor, a thoughtful look on her face. 'Why didn't anyone cut the cake?'

'Sorry?'

'The party downstairs. No one had bothered to cut the cake. And you only left the office just before me, so you didn't even have time for a party—' She stared at him as she worked it out. 'It was a surprise party, wasn't it? And you told them to get out.'

'Not all surprises are good ones. And now I'd like you to get out too.' His acid tone had no effect. She was like a barnacle, he thought, refusing to be chipped from the rock.

'I assume it was Tara and her hangers-on?' Her expression told him everything he needed to know about her opinion of the egocentric model. 'She should *not* have left you like this.'

'I ordered her to leave.'

'Then she shouldn't have listened. What was the occasion?'

'Her birthday.' He watched as her lips parted in astonishment. Soft lips, he noticed. Unpainted. She was wearing the same plain grey skirt she'd worn to work that day with a white shirt and a maroon sweater under her extremely damp coat. She looked sober and sensible. But then Emma always dressed soberly. Her hair was always smooth and neat, secured away from her face with a large clip that never failed her. She was the consummate professional in every way.

'She threw a surprise party for her *own* birthday?'

'I'd already told her this wasn't a good night for me. Tara isn't good at hearing no.'

'Why?'

Lucas gave a sardonic smile. 'Because she's a woman?'

'No—' her frown was impatient '—I mean, why isn't this a good night for you? I want to know why you're insistent on being on your own and why you're drinking your way through the entire contents of your cellar. Is it work? Has something gone wrong with the Zubran contract that I don't know about?'

'Why would you think it has anything to do with work?'

'Because work is the only thing that matters to you.'

Lucas stared at her for a long moment. Then

he turned and threw the log he was holding onto the fire. The flames licked at it greedily, consuming it and delivering a sudden flare of heat.

He couldn't blame her for thinking that, could he?

She had no idea.

And that was a good thing. The last thing he was looking for was sympathy or understanding.

'You shouldn't be here, Emma.'

'But I am here. And I might be able to help.' She stood, straight and tall. Honest. Straightforward. A woman with a heart, innocent of how dark the world could be.

He made a point of avoiding women like her. Innocence had no place in his life. He was not a good guardian of innocence. Even thinking about it made his palms begin to sweat. 'You can't help.' Their relationship had always been strictly professional. For Lucas, business and pleasure didn't mix. He'd thought she felt the same way.

'Are you upset about Tara? Is that what's wrong? This isn't like you. In all the time I've worked for you I've never seen you remotely emotional about a woman. I've come to the conclusion that they're no more than an accessory to you. A bit like your cufflinks. You wear different ones, depending on the occasion.'

It was such a perceptive comment that had he not been struggling with his black mood, he might have laughed. He certainly would have been impressed. As it was, he just wanted her gone and if she was going to ignore his request for her to leave then it was time to employ other methods.

'Maybe it is like me. Maybe you don't know what I'm like. Maybe you don't know me at all.' Lucas prowled over to her, watching as she registered the threat in his tone. And because he was watching, because he was experienced, he sensed she was struggling not to step back.

'Don't intimidate me. I'm trying to help, Lucas.'

'And I don't want help. Not yours. Not anyone's.' *If nothing else would work, then this would.* Telling himself that he was doing her a favour, he flattened her back against the exposed brick of the wall. Her shallow breathing was the only sound in the room apart from the occasional crackle from the blazing fire. Next to them a window looked down at moonlit snow but his attention was on the soft curve of her mouth. Her hair smelled of flowers and wood smoke.

His body stirred, his response to her primitive, powerful and entirely inappropriate.

Her eyes were fixed on him, wide and shocked.

And he couldn't blame her for that. He was shocked too. Shocked by the concentrated rush of raw desire that ripped through him, shocked by the degree of control he had to exert over himself to prevent himself from doing what he was suddenly burning to do.

In a few brief seconds the nature of their relationship had shifted. Here, outside the glass walls of his office, the barrier had lowered.

Not boss and employee.

Man and woman.

He hadn't expected that. He certainly didn't want it. Not tonight and not with this woman.

It was the drink, he thought. Damn the drink, because he didn't want that barrier lowered. Not just because that was a line he never crossed with someone who worked for him, but because he knew that what he had to give wasn't what she would want.

Not trusting himself to be this close to her, he was about to step back when she pushed at his chest and escaped from his grasp. 'I'll leave you to sober up.'

She seemed as brisk and efficient as ever, but Lucas knew that she wasn't. He heard the shake in her voice and saw the way her hands clutched at her wet coat as if she were trying to hold herself together.

He'd unsettled her.

Maybe he'd even scared her a little.

And that had been his intention, hadn't it? He'd wanted her to walk away.

So why, in those few tense seconds as she stalked towards the door, did he find himself noticing things he hadn't noticed before? Like the fact that her hair was the same rich glossy brown as the wood panelling in the tower bedroom and that she was one of the only women he knew who was still capable of blushing.

He found himself wondering about Jamie, the man she was rushing home to.

All he knew about the guy was that she'd been

with him for the whole time she'd worked for him. Two years. And that confirmed everything he already knew about her.

Emma believed in love.

And with that thought he reached for another bottle of champagne.

For the second time that evening, Emma stomped down the stairs into the main hallway. The only difference was that this time she was shaking. Her knees shook, her fingers shook. Even her stomach shook.

From the first day she'd taken the job, she'd tried not to think of Lucas Jackson as a man. He was her *boss*. Her employer. Someone who paid her salary. Of course she couldn't help but be aware of his appeal to women because she fielded his calls—and she fielded a *lot*—but somehow she'd managed to view his sex appeal in a detached way, a bit like admiring a valuable painting in a gallery that you knew you'd never be able to hang on your own wall.

And then suddenly, out of nowhere, had come this rush of sexual awareness that she absolutely didn't want to feel. She was happy with her life.

Happy doing her job and going home to Jamie.
She didn't want to jeopardize any of that. She
couldn't *afford* to jeopardize any of that. Especially not for a rude, totally selfish human being
like Lucas Jackson.

Sexy eyes, a great body and a brilliant mind
didn't make up for serious deficiencies in his
personality. He didn't care about anyone. And
that, she told herself firmly, was not an attractive trait.

And she was well aware that the incident back
in the cosy turret bedroom had been about control, not chemistry.

He'd been trying to unsettle her. Trying to get
her to back off. Well, that was fine. She'd backed
off, hadn't she?

But she wasn't leaving. There was no way she
could leave another human being in that state.

Trying to forget the way he'd looked at her
as he'd pinned her to the wall, Emma reached
the bottom of the stairs and stared at the decorations, so tacky and out of place in the elegant
hallway. Something about the surprise party had
upset him. Or maybe he'd been upset before he'd

arrived home. Whichever, it was the first time she'd ever seen him drunk.

Deciding that the decorations were presumably as unwelcome as the party, she set about removing them. As she liberated a streamer that had been twisted around the ornate frame of a painting, a memory came at her from nowhere.

It wasn't the first time she'd seen him drunk, was it? It was the second time. And the first time would have been—when? Trying to remember, she twisted the streamer between her fingers. There had been snow on the ground then too. It would have been around the same time of year as this.

Last year.

She'd worked late and assumed she was on her own in the building apart from Security, but when she'd walked into his office Lucas had been there, sprawled on the sofa with an empty bottle of whisky next to him.

He'd been asleep and she hadn't woken him.

Instead, she'd covered him with a blanket and checked on him a few times while she quietly got on with her work.

He probably didn't even know who had put the

blanket there. Either way, neither of them had ever referred to it.

Reaching up, she removed the rest of the streamers and the balloons.

It had been exactly this week. It might even have been the same date. She remembered because it was the same time that she took her holiday every year.

She stood, holding a bouquet of unwanted festivity as she thought it through.

Was it a coincidence that he was drunk again? Yes, probably. It was a busy time and everyone was entitled to let their hair down from time to time. Even the ruthlessly focused Lucas.

Emma clenched her jaw and stabbed the balloons with her car keys until they popped. *It was none of her business.*

But what if it wasn't coincidence that he'd chosen to drink alone on the same night last year? What if it wasn't coincidence that a man who forgot nothing chose this night to forget important documents?

She gathered up the last of the streamers until the only remaining evidence of the unwanted party was the uncut cake and the empty glasses.

With a murmur of frustration, she glanced over her shoulder towards the stairs.

This was one of those situations where she couldn't win. If she left she'd worry and if she stayed she ran the risk of being shouted at again. Or worse.

Her cheeks heated. What if he thought she'd stayed for a different reason? She wasn't stupid enough to think he hadn't noticed the way she'd reacted to him earlier. Lucas Jackson had far too much experience with women not to have noticed. Her only hope was that he was too drunk to remember. That, by morning, the single breathless moment when she'd forgotten to think of him as her boss would have been drowned out by other more important memories. And if he did happen to remember it, with luck he'd dismiss it as a figment of his imagination. A memory spun by alcohol, not reality. Her own behaviour would support that belief because at work she was always careful never, *ever* to stray into the realms of personal.

Looking out of the window, she saw that the snow was still falling.

She'd stay another half an hour, she decided.

She'd check on him one more time, hopefully without him even noticing her, just as she'd done the last time. And then she'd leave him to his snowy solitude.

CHAPTER THREE

LUCAS stood under the shower while needles of icy water stung his skin. He was undoubtedly drunk but, instead of being numbed, his senses appeared heightened. He was having thoughts he absolutely should *not* be having and he blamed that on the champagne. Thank goodness Emma had walked out when she had, otherwise he might have been tempted to seek an entirely different form of oblivion.

He gave a growl of self-disgust.

Since when had he imagined his PA naked? Never. Not once. But suddenly he found himself tormented by thoughts of dark, shiny hair. He'd wanted to yank out that damn clip and let it tumble free. He'd wanted to sink his hands into it and drown in the softness. He'd wanted to twist it around his fingers and hold her captive while he drank from that soft, innocent mouth to see if she were the cure he'd been looking for.

And he shouldn't want any of those things.

Cursing softly, he leaned his shoulders against the cool tiles, closed his eyes and let the water slide over his head.

He shouldn't want to touch her hair and he definitely shouldn't be thinking about kissing that mouth. Emma worked for him and he wanted her to continue to work for him. And there was no cure for what he was feeling.

It had been a rocky road finding someone suitable to fill the role of his personal assistant—a role that required a multitude of skills. Before Emma he'd had a series of giggling girls for whom work was nothing more than a way to fund their social life. He'd had girls who were overawed by him, girls whose only reason for working late was the wistful hope that their relationship with him might turn into something more intimate. He'd had a male PA who had sadly struggled with the sheer volume of simultaneous projects he'd been expected to handle and an older woman who was a grandmother four times over, but she hadn't had the stamina to handle the heavy workload and had resigned after a month.

And then he'd discovered Emma. Emma, with her serious brown eyes and her astonishing ability to juggle any number of projects at the same time without complaint. Emma, who never worked with one eye on the clock and had an admirable way of soothing the most frayed of tempers. She was the ultimate professional and it was that dedication to her job, her understanding of the importance of attention to detail, that had brought her out here tonight.

She was a gem.

And he'd shouted at her. And worse, he'd scared her.

His head spinning, Lucas swore under his breath and wondered if he'd remember to send her flowers when he was sober. The irony was, he never sent a woman flowers. Emma did it for him. But he'd have to do *something* because the last thing he wanted was for her to resign.

Hopefully they would both be able to ignore that single moment when their view of each other had changed and re-establish the normal parameters of their relationship.

Switching off the shower, he grabbed a towel.

He dried himself briefly and then tried to tie

the towel around his waist but his fingers were clumsy and uncoordinated so in the end he gave up and dropped the towel on the floor with a frustrated laugh directed towards himself. Too drunk to secure a towel, apparently, but not drunk enough to forget.

Never drunk enough to forget.

The pain was lodged under his ribs like shrapnel that couldn't be removed. Nothing eased the ache.

Surprised that he could still walk in a straight line, he returned to the bedroom and stopped dead because Emma was standing there.

For a moment he assumed that she was nothing more than a vivid image conjured by an intoxicating mixture of champagne, wishful thinking and inappropriate thoughts.

And then he heard a soft sound escape from her throat.

Her shocked eyes slid down his naked body and widened.

'Oh my God—' With a gurgle of horror she slapped her hand over her eyes and turned her head away. 'Sorry! I'm so *sorry*. I… What are you doing walking around naked? I can't believe you just…and I…' She broke off, hideously embarrassed, and it was that embarrassment that penetrated his fuzzy brain.

Not an image, he thought. An image wouldn't turn scarlet and have her hands over her eyes.

And he didn't trust himself to move because suddenly all he wanted to do was give in to that most primitive part of himself, throw her down on the bed and explore a different way of getting through this one night. He wanted her to be the heat that melted the chill inside him. He wanted her warmth and all that was real about her. Instead of being surrounded by ghosts, he wanted human contact. Flesh and blood. *Emma.*

Hands clenched by his sides, he channelled all his power and strength into standing still. 'I thought you'd left.'

'No! I just went downstairs to tidy up and give you some space and—' Her hand still over her eyes, she snatched in a breath. 'Are you decent yet?'

'For God's sake, Emma, stop overreacting.' Tension made his voice rougher than he intended. 'You must have seen a naked man before.' *Jamie*, he thought bitterly. *She'd seen Jamie.*

'You're my boss—' her voice was muffled '—I don't think of you as a man. Or at least I didn't until… Please can you just get dressed or something? This is *not* good.'

In other circumstances he might have smiled at her confusion, but a smile was nowhere near his grasp. Instead he walked into the small anteroom he used as a dressing room and grabbed a robe. Any benefit derived from the cold shower had been instantly wiped out by the sight of her. Raw lust mixed uncomfortably with the knowledge that this was one woman he couldn't have.

He needed to switch it off. He *had* to switch it off.

However much he'd drunk, this was *not* going to happen. She was the last woman in the world he wanted to see as—well, as a woman.

Dragging his hand through his wet hair, he prowled back into the room. 'I presume you came back to tell me you're snowed in?'

'I have no idea if I'm snowed in. I haven't tried to leave.' Her hand was still over her eyes and Lucas sighed and knotted the cord around his robe firmly. Then he closed his hands over her wrists and tugged firmly at her hands. She kept her eyes screwed tightly shut. 'Really, I don't want to—'

'I'm decent.' At least on the outside. His thoughts were far from decent but as long as she couldn't read minds, everything would be fine. Trying to ignore the warmth and softness of her skin against his palms, he let go of her wrists and stepped back for no other reason than the fact he knew he wasn't sober enough to make good decisions. *Distance*, he thought. *All he had to do was keep his distance.* 'If you're not snowed in, why are you still here? You left half an hour ago.'

'I told you, I was clearing up all those balloons and things. I assumed you didn't want them. And I was worried about you.' Cautiously, she half opened her eyes and when she saw the robe she relaxed and opened them properly. 'I was worried that you'd carry on drinking your way through all that champagne, fall face down in the fire and die a hideous death.'

'Worrying about your job again?'

'Of course.' Avoiding his gaze, she pushed strands of damp hair away from her face. 'And possibly my conscience. I want to be able to sleep at night.'

Distracted by all that lush, dark hair, Lucas found it hard to keep his mind focused. 'Maybe I'm more drunk than I think I am, but why would that be on your conscience?'

'Because I would have been the last person to see you alive.' Wrapping her arms around herself, she gave a little shrug and backed towards the staircase. 'But if you're sober enough to take a shower without drowning, I expect you're safe to be left so…I'll just go.'

He was used to her being brisk and confident in all things. He'd never seen her like this. 'Why aren't you looking at me?'

'Because I still haven't recovered from the shock of the last time I looked at you. Seeing your boss naked isn't something that happens every day of the week.' She was stammering and flustered. 'I may need therapy. And this time I really am going.' She felt for the handrail at the top of the spiral staircase, her gaze everywhere except on him even though his robe was firmly secured around his waist.

Her unsophisticated response simply fuelled

his libido and he felt a rush of frustration because what he had to do was in direct conflict with what he wanted to do. 'You're not going anywhere, Emma.' He watched as her pale throat moved as she swallowed hard.

'Yes, I am. You're obviously fine to be left so—'

'When did you last look outside?'

The tension in the air built around them. It didn't help that the turret bedroom was designed for seduction with its huge four-poster bed, flickering fire and windows that gave a perfect view of the estate. The snow reflected the moon and sent a ghostly silver light over the wood and the lake, producing a view that was both ethereal and romantic.

The irony was that he never had seduced a woman here. With the exception of Tara's impromptu, unwanted visit earlier, no woman had ever visited him at Chigworth.

But Emma was here now, and she was clearly regretting her earlier decision to stay around.

'It will be fine,' she said firmly. 'I'm good in the snow. If I drive carefully I'll be able to get to the end of the road. The gritting lorries were already working on the motorway so I shouldn't have any trouble getting home once I get to the main roads.'

'And do you know how far it is to the main roads from here? Even if you make it out of the estate, which I doubt that you would, you have five miles of country roads that are always low on the priority list for whoever decides which part of our little island is gritted in bad weather.'

'Well, I'll give it a try anyway.'

'I may be drunk,' Lucas drawled, 'but I'm not so drunk that I can't recognise a truly bad idea when I see it. Call me selfish, but I don't want to spend the rest of tonight trying to locate your frozen corpse. Nor do I want to find myself recruiting a new PA. I can't stand the interview process.'

Her lips twitched as she tried to hold back a smile. 'It's all about you, isn't it?'

'Absolutely. I'm the most selfish bastard you'll ever meet, you know that.' *So don't look at me with those soft brown eyes. Don't show me that you care.*

But she'd already done that, hadn't she? The moment she'd discovered that he hadn't wanted a party, she'd set about quietly removing the evidence.

Hands clasped in front of her, she stared at the floor. 'I was stupid, wasn't I, coming here in the first place.'

'Not stupid, no.' Because he could barely keep his hands off her, Lucas strolled over to the fire and kept his back to her. 'You were dedicated. Professional. Which is no more than I would have expected from you. It's just unfortunate that you chose tonight.' He didn't state the obvious. That if it hadn't been for what this night did to his mind, he wouldn't have forgotten the damn file in the first place.

'Lucas—'

'This is what we're going to do.' Taking control, he turned, interrupting her before she could ask the question he knew she was going to ask. *The question about why exactly this night was so painful for him.* 'You are wet, cold and, presumably, very tired. I'm going down to the kitchen to make us some soup and while I do that you are going to have a hot bath or shower—whichever—and then help yourself to whatever clothes take your fancy from my dressing room. Nothing will fit, but you're a practical enough person to improvise, I'm sure. We'll hang yours up and they'll be dry in the morning.'

'Lucas, I can't—'

'I'm going to light a fire in one of the other bedrooms, then it will be warm once you're ready to sleep.' Without looking at her, he strode towards the staircase, keeping his hands to himself. 'There are plenty of warm towels in the bathroom. Help yourself.'

She should have argued, but one glance through the pretty arched window convinced her that he was right. In the half hour she'd spent clearing up downstairs, killing time until she could check on him again, it seemed as if half a ton of fresh snow had fallen. It glistened in the moonlight, a sparkly, silvery deathtrap. The decision whether or not to stay was out of her hands. She wasn't going to be going home any time soon. She was stuck here with a man who clearly didn't want her around when all she wanted was to be home with Jamie.

What she should have done was leave when it had been possible to do so, instead of putting him in a position where he had no choice but to offer her accommodation. And if there were other feelings sloshing around inside her, then she chose to ignore them, just as she was trying to ignore the recurring images of that one dangerous glimpse of him naked.

It was a shame he wasn't flabby, she thought gloomily. A seriously out of shape boss would have been so much easier to forget than a boss with rock-hard abs and—

Emma squeezed her eyes shut and reminded herself that a luscious body didn't maketh a man.

And there was no point in going back over what she could have done or should have done because she was stuck here now so she just had to make it work.

Resigned to the inevitable, she started by calling Jamie to tell him she wouldn't be home. It was a call she dreaded making and she breathed a sigh of relief when the phone went to voice-mail.After she'd left a brief message explaining the facts and promising to call the next morning once she'd had a chance to check the weather and road conditions, she eased off her soaking-wet shoes and put them close to the fire to dry off.

Shivering now, she realised just how wet she was. Shrugging off her coat, she draped it over the back of the chair, checking it was far enough away from the fire to be safe from sparks. Then she walked towards the bathroom.

She was far too cold to argue with his suggestion that she have a hot bath. She needed to warm up and change into dry clothes.

Despite the age of the castle, the bathroom was the last word in luxury and Emma gave a moan of pleasure as she slid her freezing cold limbs into the warm, scented water. She never did this. She usually took a shower because it was faster. Everything in her life was dictated by speed and efficiency. Her life was such a crazy whirl that it was all about racing on to the next thing on her list, never about just enjoying a moment of self-indulgence. But she enjoyed it now, so tired after her week at work that she didn't dare allow herself to lie back and close her eyes for long in case she slept.

She could have stayed there for ever, but in the end stayed just long enough to thaw her frozen limbs. Then she let her hair down and lathered it clean, feeling the hot water stinging her scalp as she rinsed away the evidence of her fall in the snow.

It felt blissful to be clean and warm. Only the knowledge that if she didn't reappear he'd come looking for her was enough to eject her from the water. Grabbing two towels, Emma dried herself with one and then wrapped the other around her head. Then she popped her head round the door. Relieved that there was still no sign of him, she walked into his dressing room wondering what on earth she was likely to find to wear. A sweater would be fine, she thought. Or a shirt of some sort to sleep in. Anything, really, as long as it was decent.

Ignoring the rows of suits, she instead selected a white shirt. It would be much too big for her but she could just roll up the arms. Now all she needed was to find something to wear on her bottom half so that she didn't freeze to death or expose herself. Didn't the man own sweatpants or something? Pyjamas?

Deciding that everything on the rails was too formal, she instead focused on the drawers. Opening the top one, she found socks. Deciding that socks might be useful, she pulled out a pair and then opened the next drawer.

But Lucas Jackson didn't appear to own either pyjamas or anything suitably casual and she was just about to give up on the final drawer when her fingers brushed against something hard. Shifting aside the neatly folded T-shirt, she saw a photograph in an antique silver frame.

Wondering why a photograph would be buried in the bottom of a drawer, she picked it up. As she stared at the faces in the picture, she held her breath.

This photograph hadn't been buried by accident, she thought numbly. It hadn't tumbled there or been stowed away in a moment of decluttering. It had been hidden there intentionally by someone who couldn't bear to look at it, but equally couldn't bear to part with it. For some reason she didn't yet understand, that image represented pain.

'Emma?' Lucas's voice came from outside the bedroom and she jumped guiltily. Whether or not she would have replaced the photograph she didn't have a chance to find out because one minute she was alone with his secrets and the next he was standing in the doorway, witnessing her trespass into a private part of his life that he'd clearly labelled 'no admittance'.

His eyes flickered to the frame in her hands and the change in him was instantaneous. The colour literally drained from his face, the sudden pallor emphasising the dark shadows that lurked in his eyes. And she knew immediately that what she held in her hands held the clue to the source of those shadows. Across that narrow distance she *felt* his agony and she wanted to offer comfort but how could she when she didn't even know what she was offering comfort for? And how could she discuss something this personal with someone who didn't encourage personal? The nature of their relationship would be for ever shifted.

But it already was, she thought. Even if she said nothing, she knew now that Lucas *did* have a personal life. That he was so much more than the man she'd thought she knew.

And this was worse, far worse, than seeing him naked, she realised. This was more intimate. More intrusive. And he obviously thought so too because there was no sign now of the indifference with which he'd treated her unexpected appearance in his bedroom. No trace of amusement in those cold blue eyes. His unsmiling gaze travelled from the towel tied around her head to the towel wrapped around her body and Emma lifted her hand instinctively to the knot, even though she knew it was tied firm.

'I...I was just looking for something to wear. I didn't mean to pry.' Feeling the heat pour into her cheeks, she slid the photograph back where she'd found it. But it was too late, of course. The damage was done and it couldn't be undone. 'I'm sorry.' The words left her in a stumbled rush. 'I didn't know it was there. You told me to help myself to clothes and that was what I did, and... maybe I shouldn't have looked at it, but I didn't know it was significant until I looked and—' She broke off, waiting for him to speak, but he said nothing.

He was as cold and inhospitable as the snow and ice clinging to the trees outside, his emotions as frozen as the moat.

And Emma had no idea what she was supposed to do now. What to say. So in the end she just said the obvious thing. 'You have a daughter.' Her voice was barely audible. 'And she looks exactly like you.' And the moment she said it, she knew that the obvious thing had been the wrong thing.

The silence stretched for so long she was about to mumble an apology when he finally spoke.

'I *had* a daughter.' This time his tone wasn't harsh or angry. In fact it was oddly flat, as if all the emotion had drained out of him. 'She died, four years ago tonight, and it was my fault. She died because of me.'

CHAPTER FOUR

SHE'D found the photograph. The photograph he couldn't bear to look at.

Lucas stood by the window of the tower with his back to the room. His chest ached. He felt raw, as if his flesh had been ripped from his bones, every last layer of protection stripped from him.

He had no idea how to ease the pain.

He was a man who prided himself on his control and yet right now it was nowhere within his grasp. His hand curled into a fist and he pressed it against the wall and closed his eyes, trying to pull together the torn edges of his self-control.

From the dressing room he could hear a soft rustle as she dressed. He guessed she'd managed to find clothes but she was taking her time and it was all too easy to understand why. The expression on her face stayed with him, the impact of his raw confession a million times more shocking than the moment she'd seen him naked.

And in a way she had.

She'd seen a part of him he'd never shown to anyone else. A part of him he guarded fiercely. He had no issues with her having seen him without his clothes on. He had plenty with the fact she'd seen that photograph.

And he was willing to bet she was as appalled as he was.

It was ironic, he thought, that it had taken this to finally give him what he'd been hoping for. Solitude. Because he had no doubt that now she'd leave him alone. Given the choice of waiting out the weather in the warm bedroom downstairs or with him in his own private version of hell, he had no doubt which option she'd pick.

He was so sure that would be her choice that it was a shock to hear her soft tread on the wooden floor.

'So is this what you do every year?' Her soft voice brushed over his nerve endings. 'Shut yourself away and drink? Does that help you get through the night?'

Because he wanted her to leave, he didn't turn. 'Nothing helps.'

'No. I can imagine that it wouldn't.' He felt her sympathy and her compassion and rejected both because he knew he deserved neither.

'I appreciate your dedication in bringing the file here tonight, but your job is done, Emma.' He knew he sounded brutal but he didn't even care. 'Your responsibility doesn't extend to any other part of my life. The bedroom downstairs is warm and comfortable. I've left a tray of food there. Eat and then get some rest.'

'What about you? What will you do?'

What he always did. Put one foot in front of the other and keep on living even though others didn't. 'I'll be fine. Eat the food while it's hot.'

There was a brief pause. 'Instead of getting through it on your own, you could try another way.'

He didn't hear her move but suddenly her hand was on his shoulder. He stiffened his muscles against that gentle touch, surprised that she couldn't sense the violence in him. Or maybe she did and chose to ignore it. He knew she was no coward. If she were, she would have driven off the first time instead of coming back to check on him. 'You need to leave, Emma. Now.'

'If it's about finding ways to get through a hideous, horrible night then there has to be a better way than drinking. Or at least a way that won't have you waking up feeling even worse in the morning.'

'What better way?' He turned, slowly, the effort of fighting suddenly too much. His eyes found hers. She was wearing one of his white shirts and it fell to mid-thigh exposing a long, tempting length of leg. Part of him was clearly still functioning normally because he found himself wondering how he could possibly have missed the fact that Emma had fabulous legs and then realised that her office dress was always businesslike, never provocative. Intentional, perhaps, if this was what she was hiding under grey wool.

The inappropriateness of his thoughts almost made him laugh.

Was this really the only feeling of which he was capable? Surely it should be gratitude, or some other equally bland and harmless emotion. What he was feeling definitely wasn't harmless.

It was raw, dangerous and powerful and it threatened to burn up anything or anyone standing in his path.

And she sensed it.

He saw the exact moment she read his mood. The expression in her brown eyes shifted from warmth to something different. Her certainty seemed to falter and her hand fell from his shoulder.

A cynical smile touched his mouth. 'Exactly.' He softened his voice in an attempt to snap the tension that was brewing in the air. 'You need to be more specific when suggesting alternatives or your generosity might be misconstrued. Especially when you're wearing nothing more than one of my shirts.'

'You date women who wear nothing but designer couture. You expect me to believe that seeing your PA in one of your own shirts is going to send your libido into the danger zone? I don't think so.' Her tone was light but it was the sort of lightness that took effort to produce and her cheeks were streaked with pink. 'You're not that desperate.'

'Maybe I am.' His voice thickened by emotion that had been simmering all day, Lucas slid his hand round the back of her head and forced her to look at him. 'Maybe I'm so desperate I don't care what I do tonight. Or who I do it with. And maybe that makes this the worst place you could be right now, Emma.' He could feel her pulse galloping under his fingers. Sensed that she was afraid to breathe in case she upset the delicate balance that existed between them. She was afraid she was going to tip him over the edge and he found himself incapable of reassuring her. He'd always thought of her as sturdy and robust but the thin silk of his shirt revealed slender, flowing lines and everything fragile.

And he wasn't to be trusted with fragile, was he?

He'd already proved that.

The thought was like a shower of cold water.

His hand dropped.

Disgust was a bitter taste in his mouth. Was he really so desperate that he'd risk hurting one of the few genuine people in his life? 'You should leave. Now. Go downstairs and lock your door.' He wondered why she couldn't sense the urgency. Or was it just that she had no sense of danger?

Either way, she didn't move. 'There's no way I'm leaving you like this.'

'You should have left hours ago when I told you to and then we wouldn't have found ourselves in this position.'

'I'm glad I didn't. You shouldn't be on your own tonight.'

'Because you're worried about your job?'

'No. Because I'm worried about *you*.'

'You just don't get it, do you?' The violence in him was so close to the surface that he could taste it. He stepped towards her, her subtle perfume sliding over his senses and disturbing the balance of his control. 'I *should* be on my own. It's the only way that works.' He expected her to step back but she didn't even flinch.

'It doesn't look as if it's working to me. Perhaps it's time you considered a different way. Perhaps, instead of alcohol and oblivion, you might try friendship and comfort.'

'Friendship?' The word chafed against his raw feelings. 'You think right now I have *friendship* on my mind?'

'No. I don't think that. I'm not stupid. But I think you are hurting so badly all you want to do is make it stop. You want a rest from the pain. And I made that pain worse by finding that photograph,' she said quietly, 'and I'm sorry for that.'

'You have no reason to be sorry. Now go.'

'No. We can find another way to do this.'

He shouldn't have been surprised by her stubbornness because she showed the same indomitable spirit at work. 'There is no "we" in this, Emma. And as for friendship—' it seemed imperative to smash her illusions about that '—I don't have friends. I have people who want something from me and people who work for me.' His harsh analysis didn't seem to surprise her. *Maybe she wasn't as naïve as he thought she was.*

'You only think like that because of the company you keep. But you shouldn't judge everyone based on the actions of Tara Flynn. She shouldn't have left you alone tonight. That was wrong of her.'

At another time he would have been amused that she thought Tara capable of the sort of care she was describing. 'Perhaps she was sensible. Perhaps she realised that it wasn't safe to stay'

The heat of the fire had dried her hair curly and it tumbled in thick, dark waves over the snowy white of his shirt, which was proving woefully inadequate as a cover-up. The flickering light from the fire shone through the thin fabric, clearly outlining the dips and curves of her body and suddenly it was becoming harder and harder to do the right thing and send her away.

'It's true that I work for you. But it's wrong to dismiss that relationship as a purely economic arrangement. I've worked closely with you for two years. I care.' She bit her lip. 'I was with you this time last year when you emptied a bottle of whisky and slept in your office, although I doubt you remember.'

It came back to him instantly. The blanket. She was the one responsible for the blanket. It was a question that had bugged him on and off over the past twelve months and now he had the answer.

Emma.

She hesitated and then held out her hand. 'Stop drinking, Lucas. You've tried that and it hasn't worked. We're going to find another way to get through tonight. And before you make another caustic comment involving all sorts of physical alternatives, I should point out that there are a million other options that aren't going to make it embarrassing to bump into each other in the morning.'

'What options?' His mind had been so full of those physical alternatives that it took him a minute to focus on what she'd said.

She pursed her lips thoughtfully. 'We could play chess?'

'Chess?' Did she even realise that he could see through the shirt? No, presumably not or she wouldn't have been standing there so confidently.

'I'm a brilliant chess player.' Her fingers closed over his, soft and warm, her grip surprisingly firm.

Instead of removing his hand from hers as he should have done, Lucas found himself staring at her mouth. 'You don't want to challenge me to chess. It would end in tears.'

'*Your* tears, I presume.' A half smile tilted that mouth at the corners. 'There's no need to make excuses. If you're too scared to play, I understand. There's always Scrabble. But I should warn you that I know all the words in the Chambers dictionary containing Z and X and I'm a ruthless player. I will not hesitate to use a Q on a triple word score.'

Ruthless? He looked down at her sweet face and almost laughed. She wouldn't know ruthless if she passed it in the street. 'These are your best suggestions for distraction? Chess and Scrabble?'

'Unless you're up for an all-nighter, in which case I'm a whizz at Monopoly.'

'You think it's wise to play Monopoly with an architect?'

'Why not? If you're trying to scare me you won't succeed. If you were a building contractor, perhaps I'd be nervous of your capacity to build large hotels on your property, but an architect like yourself who is capable of nothing more impressive than pretty drawings—' she shrugged '—no challenge. So—which is it to be? Chess, Scrabble or Monopoly? Do you want to play?'

Yes, he wanted to play.

But none of the games she was suggesting. The

game he wanted to play was far, far more dangerous. He wanted to play with fire. He wanted to kiss that mouth, strip off that shirt that barely covered her and seek oblivion in the most basic way known to man. And he wanted to do it again and again until his mind was wiped of everything except her. Until he forgot. Until the pain was drowned out by other sensations.

Why not? Nothing else had worked. Nothing else had helped.

And then he remembered that this was Emma.

And that she was absolutely and completely off-limits.

He forced himself to extract his hand from hers. 'I've never met anyone who could beat me at chess,' he said coldly, 'and I can't think of anything worse than property development with toy money. I put a bowl of soup in your room. If it isn't enough then help yourself to anything you find in the kitchen.' He turned his back to her and waited to hear the outraged tap tap of her footsteps retreating towards the stairs as she responded to his rude rejection.

Instead he felt her arms come round his waist. 'I don't know what happened,' she said hesitantly, 'but I know it couldn't have been your fault. I *know* that. She didn't die because of you.'

Something inside him snapped. 'You don't know anything.' His voice savage, he turned so violently that her hands dropped. 'You have no idea what you're talking about and you have to leave this alone. You have to leave *me* alone.' Somehow his head was close to hers, his stance so threatening that she should have instantly backed off but she didn't move.

'I won't leave you alone.'

'No? Then maybe this will change your mind. There is only one other form of distraction I'm willing to try. Are you willing to play that game, Emma?' Somehow his hands had buried themselves in her hair, the softness of it engulfing his fingers and flowing over his wrists. Without pause or hesitation he took her mouth, his kiss rough and demanding, hard against soft, bitter against sweet. He was driven not just by lust, but by desperation. By some deep, primitive need to try and drive out the agony that possessed him. He was drawn to her warmth, as if being close to her might somehow melt the thick layer of ice inside him. As if something in her might be able to heal that damaged part of him even though everything else had failed. He took greedily, selfishly, ruled by his feelings, by the pain, by the need to seek oblivion wherever it was offered. He could feel her shivering against him and he had no idea if she was cold or whether some other more complicated emotion was responsible for the tremors. His thinking wasn't clear enough to make sense of it. All he knew was that he wanted this and he wanted it right now and, unless she stopped him, he wasn't stopping.

His mouth still on hers, one hand still in her hair, he used his free hand to untie his robe. Still kissing her, he shrugged it off and when her arms came round his neck he scooped her off her feet and lowered her to the rug in front of the fire. Part of him, a small distant part that had virtually no voice in the madness that engulfed him, told him to slow down, to take his time, to think of her—but there was only him and the madness inside him. He didn't want to think of her. He didn't want to think of anything.

He wasn't interested in a slow seduction.

With hands that shook, he ripped the shirt

from neck to hem, exposing her completely. Somewhere in the depths of the madness that streaked through him he heard her gasp but he blocked that out as he parted her thighs.

'Lucas—' She whispered his name and he lifted his head, his vision hazy as he tried to focus on her.

The warmth of the fire had given her cheeks a rosy glow, or perhaps she was embarrassed by the intimacy with which he touched her. Either way, her body offered up a sinuous, sensual invitation, an erotic escape from his own painful brand of reality. But even in forgetting, there was one thing he remembered, and that was to grope in his robe for the contraception that had never once been out of his reach for the past five years.

His mouth was hungry on hers and then he slid his hand down her sleek body, losing himself in her curves and her softness. His touch was bold and explicit, the sexual urge so shockingly powerful that it drove aside every other emotion and drowned out the ache. Part of him knew that he was taking this too fast, but she was like a drug. The more he consumed the better he felt and the better he felt the more he wanted. He was out of control and he knew it. He knew it as he spread her legs and heard her soft intake of breath. He knew it as he slid his hand under her and lifted her and he knew it as he thrust into her body, propelled by an almost desperate urgency that didn't allow him to hold back.

Heat engulfed him. A heat intensified a thousand times by the tightness of her body gripping his shaft. He felt every ripple of her body in the most intimate way possible. Never before had he experienced anything like it.

'God, Emma—' Her body clasped his and he wanted to pause, to make it last and prolong the moment, but he couldn't hold back. Physically he was stronger than her. Much stronger. And he used that strength as he surged deep. Through the heat that blurred his brain he heard her moan his name. Felt her fingers grip his back and heard the breath catch in her throat. Perhaps he should have slowed things, whispered soft words or gentle endearments but Lucas could no longer access soft or gentle. He was deaf and blind to everything except his own need. He felt slick silken muscle tightening around him and he gave into it, gave into the rhythm and the wildness, his performance driven by instinct, not technique. Everything about it was raw and primitive, each sure thrust of masculine possession designed for his own gratification. The bite of his hand on her soft skin held her where he wanted her. The scent of her made him dizzy and the softness of her skin drove him wild. He took greedily, he plundered all that she offered and more and, in that single moment, those few suspended seconds of sexual oblivion, he was aware of nothing but the pleasure of release. And as his body emptied, so did his brain. Emptied of everything except this woman.

It took a while for reality to return.

Lucas became aware first of the heat of the fire burning his skin, and finally of the warmth of the woman still wrapped around him. Not any woman, he thought.

Emma.

Emma, his PA. Sweet Emma who deserved so much more than a one-night stand with a selfish bastard like him.

Closing his eyes, he rolled away from her onto his back feeling a rush of self-disgust, wondering what insanity had possessed him. More alcohol would have been a better option. At least then he would have woken in the light of day with no apologies owing. There would be a price, he thought. There was always a price for everything.

The only question was how high it would be this time.

Emma woke to find herself alone in the huge four-poster bed. The first fingers of cold winter daylight shone through the windows and all that remained of the fire in the hearth that had warmed their night of loving was a sprinkle of glowing embers.

It was morning, the dawn of another day, the agony and anguish of the night before nothing more than a cold memory.

But it wasn't all forgotten, was it?

Her body ached in ways that were new to her. She felt—

Emma rolled onto her back and stared up at the canopy of the four-poster bed.

Incredible. She felt incredible. And with that thought came guilt. It seemed thoroughly wrong that what felt like the best night of her life had been the worst night of his.

For him, it hadn't been special, had it? It hadn't really been about *her* at all, even though it had been her name he'd spoken in the heat of the moment. She wasn't foolish enough to pretend it had been personal. For him, it had been nothing more than a temporary escape. She'd offered distraction at a time when he'd needed it most, a woman who'd happened to be there when he was in trouble. She was his employee—

Emma's smile vanished and she felt a sudden rush of panic as reality bloomed.

Oh God, she'd slept with her boss. What had she been *thinking*?

Sleeping with the boss wasn't incredible, it was stupid.

Stupid, stupid, stupid.

She, of all people, knew just how foolish that was. How could she have been so reckless? She was always professional. *Always*. She was always careful not to step over that line.

Emma shot out of bed on legs that shook and grabbed the clothes she'd left drying in front of the fire. Afraid that he might reappear at any moment she dressed in a flash, a surprising achievement considering that her hands were shaking as much as her legs. Switching on her phone, she saw that it was eight a.m. And she already had five missed calls from Jamie.

Oh God, *Jamie.*

It was like a thump in her stomach. The warm glow that had surrounded her when she'd woken had vanished and all that was left was cold panic.

What had she done? From the moment she'd put her hand on Lucas's shoulder, she hadn't given her life a single thought. It had all been about the moment, not about what would happen afterwards. With a groan of remorse, she sank onto the edge of the bed.

'This looks like a serious case of morning-after regret to me.' A dark male drawl came from the doorway and Emma gave a start because she'd been hoping for some time to pull herself together before having to face him and now there was no hope of that.

This was a scenario she'd never had to handle before and she was clueless.

She looked at him and felt her stomach drop. He was insanely attractive. Not just good-looking, but truly gorgeous in a deliciously sexy, bad boy sort of way, with those strands of dark hair flopping over his forehead and his jaw unshaven. Was it wrong to wish he hadn't decided to leave the bed before she woke? Wrong to wish they'd woken together?

Sex with him had been unforgettable.

And that was the problem.

He was her boss. She *had* to forget it. She had to ignore that tiny, ridiculous part of her that just wanted to resign on the spot and see if this thing between them could go somewhere. She had to ignore that part of her that wanted to forget the professional so that they could pursue the personal. That would have been crazy and impulsive and she was neither of those things. She had responsibilities. Commitments. She always made sensible decisions and the sensible decision was to lock last night away in her brain and forget it had ever happened. She had to forget everything personal that she knew about him.

The question was—*how?*

She wondered if he was asking himself the same question but one glance at his face told her that he wasn't. There was no doubt or uncertainty there. Nothing that suggested that what they'd shared had meant anything to him but a way of getting through a bad time. There was no evidence now of the unspeakable agony she'd witnessed the night before. Whatever dark, savage emotions had gripped him in the bitter cold of the night had been chased away by the morning light. Lucas Jackson was back in control, those secrets buried deep under layers of self-discipline.

She, however, felt emotionally and physically wrecked.

He was already dressed, in black jeans and a black sweater that added emphasis to powerful shoulders. His choice of clothes was casual, and yet there was still an innate sophistication about him, an effortless style that was evident in everything he did.

Through her moment of panic came the memories. Memories of how those shoulders had felt under her fingers, the ripple of male muscle and hard strength. Memories of how it had felt to touch him and be touched. Strange, she thought, how even that unscheduled glimpse of vulnerability hadn't seemed like weakness. There was nothing weak about this man.

They hadn't even talked about it, she realised. Not really. All she knew was that he blamed himself for the death of his daughter. Other than that she had no details and, judging from the grim set of his mouth, he had no intention of offering any.

This was the man she knew. The Lucas Jackson she recognised. And of course that made it worse, because *this* man was her boss.

Which really only left her with one course of action.

Emma stood up slowly, as if by taking her time a miracle might happen and she might somehow know what to say. And he was obviously waiting for her to speak. That intense blue gaze, always more perceptive than most people's, held hers for longer than was comfortable. And although it seemed shallow to care about such things, she was acutely conscious of how appalling she must look. She had that exhausted, gritty-eyed feeling that followed a night of seriously reduced sleep so she knew she'd be pale. And she knew she'd look rumpled because, although she'd pulled on clothes, she hadn't had time to do more than smooth her hair and after the way he'd treated it the night before it tumbled in a wild mess over her shoulders.

As awkward moments went, this one reigned supreme.

'Hi. Good morning—' Oh God, this was *awful*. She cleared her throat, thinking that it was impossible to sound businesslike when faced with a man who had intimate knowledge of every part of your body. 'I just need to make a quick phone call and then I'll be out of your way.'

The last thing she wanted was to talk about what had happened, so she was relieved when he said nothing. Instead, he continued to study her as if he were seeking an answer to something. And Emma soon discovered that his scrutiny was every bit as uncomfortable as any conversation would have been. The way he was looking at her unsettled her so badly that in the end she turned away and rescued her shoes from their place in front of the fire. The snow had made a mess of them, but at least they were dry and putting them on gave her something to do and made her feel more *dressed*, somehow.

Wanting to escape as fast as possible, knowing that she was already going to be in trouble, she dug her hand in her bag and pulled out her phone. 'I need to call Jamie,' she muttered, 'and tell him I'll be back later. He'll be worried that I didn't make it home last night. He's already called this morning but my phone was off.'

'Are you sure he'll be worried? You're that close, are you?' His hard tone held a hint of scepticism and she looked up, shocked and confused by the question.

Was this just about the fact he was annoyed with her for staying when he'd wanted to be alone? Was he cross that he'd woken to find that someone was the wrong side of his castle moat?

'Of course. I did tell him I'd be late but he wasn't expecting me to not make it home at all.'

Those blue eyes didn't shift from her face. 'And how is he going to feel when he finds out you had sex with me?' His blunt question was so unexpected she gave a soft gasp.

'Well, obviously I won't be mentioning that part.'

One dark eyebrow lifted and the faintest of smiles touched his hard mouth. That same mouth that had kissed her to oblivion the night before. *The same mouth that had caressed its way down her shivering, compliant body.* 'If that's your plan then you'd better learn not to blush or he'll see right through you.'

Suddenly she was angry with him. And yes, with herself. It was embarrassingly unsophisticated to have a morning-after encounter with a face the shade of a tomato, especially when he seemed to be treating the whole episode with something that came close to indifference. No romantic words then, she thought numbly. No soft smiles or gentle touches to smooth the transition from passionate to professional. And maybe she should be grateful for that, Emma thought, as she strived to match his detached approach. She would have liked to look calm and businesslike and sail out of his life with her dignity intact but she knew there was very little chance of that. 'Jamie doesn't think the way you do.'

'No?' His expression revealed nothing of his thoughts. 'What if you're wrong? What if he guesses?'

'Why would he guess? It's not exactly the sort of thing we talk about.'

'And yet you claim to be close?'

'We're close but I'm hardly going to tell him I slept with you, am I?'

'I'm no expert on relationships, but I can imagine that would make things pretty awkward.' His tone was scrupulously polite, as if they were in the office discussing a project. 'And if that's the way you want to play it, that's fine with me. But I do have one question before we turn to more practical matters.'

Practical matters? 'What question?'

There was silence, and that silence stretched from seconds to a full minute. A full minute that she counted out with each beat of her heart. And not once in that time did he stop looking at her. Not once did his gaze flicker from hers.

When he finally broke that silence, his voice was soft. 'If your relationship with Jamie is "close",' he drawled, 'why did you have sex with me?'

CHAPTER FIVE

HE WATCHED as the colour deepened in her cheeks. On one level she fascinated him because everything about her was fresh and unexpected. Or perhaps it was just that he was jaded and cynical. Too jaded and cynical for someone like her. If circumstances had been different then perhaps, just perhaps, the conversation they were about to have would also have been different. But he couldn't change the way he felt. Or rather, the way he didn't feel.

If he hadn't already regretted the madness that had driven him to take what she'd offered in the dark of the night then he regretted it now because it was all too easy to guess how she was feeling. It was written all over her face.

For her, it hadn't been about living in the moment. It had been significant. And if there was one thing he didn't look for in a relationship, it was significance. He was quite possibly the worst man she could have found herself trapped with in a snowstorm. And perhaps she knew that because right now she wasn't looking at him. All he could see was her profile. The curve of her cheeks, slightly pinker than usual, the swoop of those dark eyelashes as she focused her gaze on the snowy landscape that isolated them as effectively as any moat.

It was up to him to unravel the mess.

'Emma?' He kept his voice neutral, knowing that the way he played the next few minutes was crucial. He didn't want her to misinterpret what had happened between them. He didn't want her yearning for something that wasn't going to happen. Most of all he didn't want her ending her relationship over it, even if that relationship seemed pathetically lacking to him. 'Emma?' He repeated her name more firmly and this time she turned, her expression confused.

'I don't really understand your question.'

Which left him with no choice but to take over both sides of the conversation. 'Jamie. You've been with him for two years so it must be serious.'

She was eyeing him as if he were an alien. 'I

think there's been a bit of a misunderstanding,'
she said slowly and Lucas frowned because he
knew there was no 'misunderstanding'.

He was plain-speaking to the point of blunt
and he saw no reason to modify that trait now.
Determined to extract the truth, he took her face
in his hands, feeling the soft skin of her cheeks
against his rough palms, noticing for the first
time the flecks of green in her brown eyes.

'He's obviously someone who means a lot to
you if you've been together for two years.' He
heard the cynicism in his own voice and thought
bitterly that he had to stop judging other people's
relationships. What did he know about sustaining a long-term partnership? About as much as
he knew about love. Which was precious little.
His hands dropped to his sides.

Someone like him shouldn't be touching her.
He shouldn't have touched her the night before
and he shouldn't be touching her now.

It was wrong on every level.

She was looking at him steadily. 'I've been
with him longer than two years. Jamie and I
have been together for nine years. Which is basically the whole time he's been alive. Jamie is

my little brother. His current obsession is Star Wars Lego.'

It took a moment for those words to sink in. Brother? *Brother?*

'Lucas?' She was still watching him. Carefully, as if his every reaction was a mystery to her. 'I don't know where you got the idea Jamie was my—I don't know—significant other. You were the one who mentioned him earlier, so I assumed you knew who he was. It didn't occur to me that I needed to explain.'

'I heard you on the phone to him and—' Lucas breathed deeply and dragged his hand over the back of his neck as he confronted the depth of his error. 'Your *brother*?'

'Yes.'

'How can you have a brother who is nine years old?'

There was a hint of humour in her eyes. 'I think you can probably work that out for yourself.'

'But you're—'

'Twenty-four. And he's a lot younger than me. Welcome to the world of complicated families.' She shrugged. 'Jamie lives with my sister and me. Or rather, he lives with my sister and I join them at weekends and holidays.'

'But you live in London.'

'During the week. On Friday nights I drive to them and take over so that Angie—that's my sister—can have some time to herself. We're sort of sharing the parenting. I suppose you could say I'm the main breadwinner.'

And with that simple statement it all fell into place.

Suddenly he understood her rule that she wouldn't work on a Friday and never at a weekend. He realised how much he'd assumed and just how wrong he'd been. 'I thought you kept your weekends free because you were having a wild social life.'

'You must be confusing me with Tara,' she said lightly. 'I'm a normal person, with a normal person's life. A life that I happen to like very much. But I confess it isn't full of parties. It's a pretty routine existence.'

Lucas was stunned. 'Caring for your little brother isn't exactly a routine existence. It's an enormous sacrifice on your part.'

Her gaze cooled. 'It's not a sacrifice at all. I

consider myself very lucky to have such a lovely family. I just wish we could live in the same place all the time. It's pretty lonely for me during the week stuck in London by myself.'

'I've offended you and I apologise; it's just that I thought—' He broke off, reminding himself that his own thoughts were irrelevant. His life experience was irrelevant too. He came from a background where family ties were seen as something to be cut with a sharp blade. 'Never mind what I thought. So if you're lonely, why can't you live in the same place as them? Why London? Enlighten me.'

'We can't afford a big enough place in London, and I can't afford to work out of London because the pay isn't good enough, so this is our compromise.' She tucked a strand of hair behind her ear. 'Angie is a teaching assistant, which means she can be there for after-school care and holidays when I'm not around. It works well. Or at least, it did.'

'You mean until you got snowed in because your selfish boss kept you late at the office.'

'That wasn't really what I meant, no. Lately

it's been—' She broke off and smiled. 'Never mind. None of that is relevant.'

Lucas cursed softly and paced back to the fireplace. 'Why the hell didn't you tell me? I had no idea you had responsibility for your brother. I'm not such a monster that I would have kept you that late in the office every night if you'd explained.'

'There was nothing to explain. You pay me to do a job, and you pay me well. You have a right to expect the job done well. And I don't need to leave early during the week. I rent a room in an area of south London that couldn't exactly be described as a hub of activity. There's not a lot to go back to and anyway, I love my job.'

He dimly remembered her saying that to him the night before. 'Where exactly do you live?'

When she told him, Lucas didn't even bother trying to hide how appalled he was. 'If I'd known that I never would have let you work until two in the morning.'

'You always arranged for me to have a lift home so it was never a problem.'

'You still had to walk from the car to your house.' And the thought of her doing that horrified him. She could have been mugged. Or worse.

'You're overreacting. More often than not the driver would wait until I put my key in the door, but honestly, Lucas, I was fine.'

He looked at her cheeks, pale as chalk, and knew she wasn't fine now.

And not because of some random mugger who had attacked her in the street, but because of him. And he was about to make it a thousand times worse. He wasn't about to offer up soft words and promises of happy ever afters. He wasn't about to give her anything except a major dollop of pain.

What they'd shared was the sexual equivalent of a hit-and-run.

'We have to talk about last night.' His voice was rougher than he intended and she looked as uncomfortable as if he'd just suggested she strip naked and pose for him.

And she'd already done that.

He had a vivid image of her body, creamy skin warmed by the firelight, her curves both a sensual invitation and a balm to a man seeking oblivion.

He no longer had to wonder what she looked like under her ultra conservative clothing. He knew. *And he had to wipe it from his mind.*

'Honestly, I'd rather not.' Her hands were clasped in front of her, her knuckles white. 'Just tell me whether you want me to hand write the letter now or type it up and email it to you.'

Lucas dragged his mind away from thoughts that could only be described as shocking. 'What letter?'

'My letter of resignation. Or I suppose you could lend me a computer and I can just type it here if you like.'

'Resignation?' It was the last thing he'd expected her to say. 'What are you talking about? Why would you resign?'

'Er...because that's the only option?'

'Well, it's not an option that works for me,' Lucas thundered, the sudden rush of anger surprising him almost as much as her unexpected proposal. His emotions were all over the place and that shocked him too because he wasn't used to having to struggle for control. Usually it wasn't concealing emotion that was his problem, it was expressing it. 'I don't know why you would even suggest it when you've just spent five minutes telling me how much you love your job and how much you need the money. You're not resigning and that's final.'

Her eyes widened. 'That's my decision.'

'Well, you're making the decision for the wrong reasons so I'm not accepting it.'

'You honestly think we can still work together after last night?'

'Yes. Because last night was a one-off and is never going to happen again.' He knew from experience that it was better to spell it out but if he'd expected her to wilt then again she surprised him.

'I know that. But knowing that doesn't make it any easier to work together. It would be horribly, hideously awkward. It's already horribly, hideously awkward and since you obviously prefer to be blunt about the whole thing, I'll be blunt too. I cannot believe I had sex with my boss. I cannot believe I was so unprofessional.' She fiddled with the edge of her sweater and then turned away from him but Lucas wasn't having that.

'Why are you blaming yourself?' He closed

his hands around her shoulders and spun her round to face him, forcing her to look at him. 'What happened last night was my responsibility, not yours.'

'That isn't true. You didn't know what you were doing.' She looked pale and tired and suddenly he remembered the nightmare drive she'd had to reach him the night before. That alone must have been exhausting. And then there had been everything that had happened afterwards.

He gave a humourless laugh. 'Emma, I knew *exactly* what I was doing.' *Escaping.* Taking ruthless advantage of a decent young woman who ordinarily wouldn't have found herself anywhere near a man as damaged as him.

'It *was* my fault. You were out of your mind with grief,' she said softly. 'I handled it badly.'

'No, you didn't.'

'You told me to go away. Over and over again you told me to go. And did I listen? No, of course not.' Her tone was loaded with self-recrimination. 'It was so arrogant of me to think I could help. Stupid. There was nothing that could have helped, I see that now.'

'You did help.' And that had come as a surprise. For those moments in front of the flickering fire, the pain had eased. But at what cost? Guilt gnawed at him. 'I owe you an apology.'

'For what?'

'I used you.' His brutal honesty made her flinch.

'That isn't the way I see it.'

'Well, it's the way it was.' He refused to gild the truth and when she tried to pull away he tightened his grip, refusing to let her duck the subject. With that in mind he asked the question that had been playing on his mind since waking. 'I was rough. Did I hurt you?'

'No! You were amazing. The whole thing was incredible. To be wanted like that and—oh God, I can't believe I just said that—' She covered her face with her hands, her moan muffled. 'Please, just shoot me right now. Shoot me and end this. This has to be the single most embarrassing moment of my life. Please—if you're a nice man you'll accept my resignation and then I'll never have to face you again.'

There was something so hopelessly endearing about her that had the situation not been so serious, he would have smiled. 'I'm not a nice man and you'll be facing me on a daily basis, so you might as well get used to it.' He tugged her hands away from her face. 'And because I'm not a nice man I'm going to embarrass you even more by asking when you last had sex with someone.'

'That is *such* a personal question—' And then she caught the ironic lift of his eyebrow and turned vivid scarlet. 'You're thinking that we've already made this personal—'

'Just a little.' He made a concerted effort to delete thoughts of the way her lithe, naked body had felt under his. 'So when?'

'I don't know. It's been a while.'

Which confirmed all his worst fears. 'Why?'

'Meeting people isn't as easy as it looks in the movies. During the week I only meet people at work and I don't want to have a relationship with someone I work with—' she caught his eye and turned fiery red '—and before I took the job with you...well, there *was* someone actually,' she admitted reluctantly, 'but it didn't work out and that's probably a good thing because although I thought I was in love with him, it turned out I wasn't.'

Love.

Hearing the word was enough to make him release her but she looked so miserable that he felt the need to lighten the atmosphere. 'So let me guess—you met this loser at school and when he fumbled under your skirt you hit him with your pencil case and after that he could never father children.' He was rewarded by a gurgle of laughter.

'Close.'

'It was a school bag and not a pencil case?' Tara would have been bitching about how tired she was, he thought. He would have been treated to sulks and moods, not a sweet smile. And never in a million years would Tara have let him see her without make-up.

'It was a little more mundane than that. And it wasn't at school. I didn't have time for boys when I was at school.' Avoiding his gaze, she turned back to the window, staring down at the acres of parkland and woodland that wrapped itself around the castle. 'I was fourteen when Mum got pregnant. When other girls were discovering make-up and dating, I was helping with a baby.'

'Why? Where was your mother?'

'She died.' Slowly, she turned her head, her eyes uncertain as she looked at him. 'This is way too much information. Do you honestly want to hear it?'

'Yes.' Lucas surprised himself by saying that. 'All of it.'

She gestured awkwardly. 'It's just that we don't normally do the whole personal conversation thing—'

'Well, we're doing it now. I think we've already overstepped what might be considered personal boundaries and we've definitely passed the point of worrying about what we normally do,' he said dryly, 'so just talk. I want to know what happened.'

She paused. 'Mum found out that she was pregnant, and it was…difficult. For all of us. She was a single parent. My dad left when I was a baby so it was just her and us. And then Jamie.'

'So Jamie's dad isn't your father?' *Relationships,* he thought. *Always complicated.*

'No. And Jamie's father…well, he wasn't around either.' She didn't look at him. 'And then, neither was my mum. Five days after the birth she had a pulmonary embolism—a blood clot that lodged in her lung. Something to do with the birth and the hospital missed it.' She leaned her forehead against the window and stared down at the snow. 'She died when Jamie was just days old. And that was really…hard.' That single word encapsulated so much unspoken emotion.

He tried to imagine how that must have felt— to be fifteen and rushing home to care for a baby at a time when she was still a child herself. 'How the hell did you manage?'

'My grandparents moved in with us for a few years, and that was the worst time of all. When they first found out Mum was pregnant, they were horrified and they said so. Truthfully, they were vile to her.' Her composure slipped slightly, exposing a seam of anger. 'Then when she died they couldn't separate how they felt from the way they reacted to Jamie. They saw Jamie as the reason she was dead and it was just horrible. It was obvious that they just saw him as a mistake and a burden. That's why I snapped at you just now. That was exactly the word they used. "Sacrifice". They told us that Mum had ruined everyone's lives and if we kept Jamie we'd be throwing our lives away. They wanted us to put

him up for adoption. They didn't want him—
their own flesh and blood. Can you believe that?'

Lucas felt the ache in his temples. The pressure.

Yes, he could believe that.

'But you refused.'

'It was a hideous time. My sister and I decided
to consult a lawyer and after a long, complicated
battle which I don't intend to bore you with, we
were given custody.'

'Long and complicated?' Another understatement, he thought, oddly disturbed by the thought
of two teenage girls taking on the world in order
to keep their baby brother with them.

'We had to show we were able to care for him.
Fortunately there was money from Mum's life
insurance. My sister gave up her plans to go to
college and instead became a teaching assistant
at a school with a crèche.'

'And your grandparents?'

She rubbed her forehead with her fingers, her
expression resigned. 'Let's just say it's a tense
relationship. For Jamie's sake we wanted it to
work out but life doesn't always happen the way
you want it to.'

And didn't he know it. 'I had no idea you had such a complicated history. You never mentioned it.'

'Why would I mention it? My private life isn't exactly relevant to the practise of architecture.'

'And no doubt you're about to tell me that this man you met, who was probably the love of your life, dumped you because you had a baby to care for?'

'Actually *I* dumped *him*. He was putting so much pressure on me to lead my own life and didn't seem able to understand Jamie *is* my life. Not my whole life, obviously, but a huge part of it. As for Edward being the love of my life—' She broke off and shrugged. 'For a while I thought he was, but I was wrong. I could never love someone who had such a casual attitude towards responsibility.'

'What about since then? Are you telling me you haven't dated?'

'As I said, the only place I meet people is at work and I'd never date anyone from work.' Her smile was a rueful acknowledgement of the contradiction offered by their current position. 'Which leads me neatly back to the place we started. Lucas, you have to accept my resignation.'

'No.' He heard the ice in his own voice. 'That is not going to happen. And I can't believe you'd even suggest it.'

'We are not going to be able to work together after this.'

'Yes, we are.'

'I am not going to be able to face you on a Monday morning knowing that we…that you… you're my *boss*!'

'It was just one night, Emma. Just one night.'

'You don't have to repeat yourself. Nor do you have to panic. I don't want a relationship any more than you do.'

The fact that she read him so well should have reassured him, but it didn't. 'If you don't want a relationship then I don't understand the problem. We carry on as before. Nothing has changed.'

'Except that I've seen you naked and you've seen me naked. I just think that working with you is going to be *so* embarrassing.' Pink-faced, she wrapped her arms around herself and he found himself watching every movement she made, aware of her in a way he'd never been before. He'd worked with her for two years but he'd never really seen her.

Or maybe he hadn't allowed himself to see her.

'Then get over it. And get over it fast because I'm afraid I'm going to ask something more of you. I want you to delay the start of your holiday until at least Tuesday.'

'What?' Appalled, she stared at him. 'No way! You can't do that. I promised Jamie I'd be home. This is my holiday.'

'You can still have your holiday, it will just start a few days later.'

'But why? It's not as if you need me. You're not even in the office for the next week or so. You're in Zubran.'

'I need you with me.' He'd made the decision when he'd woken and realised what lay ahead of him. And that had been another decision that hadn't been easy to make. For personal reasons, it would have been best to send her away. For professional reasons, he needed her there.

Her mouth fell open in shock. 'You want me to go with you to *Zubran*? The desert?'

'Desert and coast. Palm trees. Sand. *Sun.* All those rare things you are unlikely to find here in a typical British winter. Or a typical British summer if it comes to that. No more shivering. Just for a couple of days.' He hadn't expected her to argue because Emma never argued with him. Usually she anticipated what he needed and provided it with smooth efficiency. 'And although you'll be working for most of the time, there should also be some downtime when you can chill by the pool.' *But not with me.* 'And do some reading or something. While I work.'

'Would you mind not emphasising the whole "one-off" thing all the time. I get it, OK? You don't have to attach a caveat to everything you say. It's very demeaning. As if you think I've suddenly turned into a creepy stalker.'

'I was just trying to tell you that as well as work, you should be able to have some time for relaxation.' Even as he said it, he wondered if she even knew the meaning of the word. It sounded as if her life had been one long slog since her early teens. 'The meeting is tomorrow and the launch party is on Sunday night. In between I have to fit in media interviews. I want you to coordinate those.'

'I know about the meeting. That's why I drove

here with those papers that need your signature. And I know about the party—I've been talking to Avery Scott about nothing but that party for the past six months. I can recite the guest list. I can itemize the menu.'

'Which is precisely why I need you there.'

'You want me at the *party*?' She looked puzzled and then surprised. 'I assumed you meant that you wanted me to deal with the media and attend the meeting.'

'That too. I had an email from the Ferrara Group this morning. They want to talk about another possible development on Sicily. They've found a piece of land that interests them in a different part of the island and want to talk through ideas.'

'Yes, I get all that—' her head throbbed at the thought of yet more work '—but why would you want me at the party? It's a social event.'

'It isn't a social event for me; it's an opportunity to showcase our work, talk to prospective clients and answer questions about the hotel structure and design. Attending alone isn't an option.'

'You were taking Tara.'

'Tara and I are finished.'

'Oh—I'm sorry.'

And that, he thought, encapsulated the difference between them because he wasn't sorry. He wasn't sorry at all. He ended relationships frequently and not once had he cared enough to be sorry.

But judging from her expression she was sorry enough for both of them, concern evident in her gaze. 'Were you in love with her?'

'No.' He didn't soften his answer. 'And she wasn't in love with me. I pick women who aren't interested in love because that is something I can't offer.'

'Presumably you must have liked *something* about her, but I must admit you don't look broken-hearted.'

'I don't have a heart, Emma. I'm sure you've heard that about me.'

'You're doing it again—delivering warnings, as if I need to be constantly reminded that last night was just one night. I'm going to have a T-shirt printed "I know it was just one night". That would cause a stir in the office.' She smiled and that smile made him catch his breath. Once again he was reminded that, although she looked delicate, she was never anything but robust.

'I apologise,' he murmured. 'I won't mention it again.'

'Good, because I can assure you that I don't want this to be more than one night any more than you do. I just want to get back to how things were before. I was just checking that you weren't upset about the whole Tara thing.'

'I'm not upset.' Nor was he used to people caring whether he was upset. He didn't tell her about the text he'd received from Tara, apologising, begging him to take her to the party. He didn't tell her that after last night he wouldn't have taken Tara if she were the last woman on earth. He didn't tell her that in all the relationships he'd had, he'd never once been upset when they'd ended.

He didn't tell her that there was something missing in him.

'She'll be disappointed not to have the opportunity to talk to all those famous people.' In that one simple sentence she summed up Tara's driving ambition. 'But I still don't see why you need me. We both know that in a room of glamorous women you'll be alone for all of five seconds.'

'I won't be alone. You'll be there.'

She shot him a look. 'Please don't ask me to do this. Not just because of the whole sex thing, but because my family is expecting me home. Angie has plans for tonight and Jamie needs me.'

'I need you.' It didn't occur to him to compromise because when it came to work he never did. He did what was best for the business. 'You drove here through a snowstorm last night to deliver me the papers I need so don't tell me you don't care about things being done well, because I know you do. It's the reason you're still working for me after two years.'

'So you're willing to take advantage of my work ethic? That isn't fair. Jamie has his school nativity play on Wednesday. Nothing is going to stop me going.'

'Fine. I'll fly you home on Monday in the jet, but you'll be exhausted because the party won't finish until the early hours.'

'Have you considered that this might backfire on you? The only party I've been to in the last few years is when our neighbours invite us in for drinks on Christmas Eve. To even call it a party is probably being over-generous. I'm not really a party person.'

'That doesn't matter.'

'*I will embarrass you!* I can look nice, but not glamorous.'

He thought about the way she'd looked lying on the rug, her hair gleaming in the red glow from the fire, and knew she was wrong, but he didn't want to say that to her because he knew he shouldn't even be thinking it. 'I'm not asking you to dance or win a fashion contest, I'm asking you to stand by my side as another representative of Jackson and Partners. It's networking. For me the party is as much business as the meeting scheduled to take place before it. You talk to many of these people on a daily basis. People speak to you before they speak to me. It's good for you to put faces to names and good for other people to know you. For many people you're their first contact with my company.'

Torn by conflicting responsibilities, she gave him an exasperated look. 'I can't believe you're asking me to do this. It's unreasonable.'

Lucas didn't relent. He told himself that if she was angry towards him that was good. Hopefully that anger would supplant other, far more dangerous, feelings and the truth was he did need her there. 'I've never claimed to be reasonable.'

'You're supposed to be embarrassed. You're ruthless, self-centred and uncaring.'

'Yes.' He didn't waste time apologising for it, nor did he tell her anything about the events that had made him that way.

She sighed. 'I don't know anything about Zubran. I can barely put it on a map.'

'What do you want to know? It's a Sultanate. A peaceful, progressive country, mostly due to the influence of the Crown Prince. Mal is superbright and very charismatic. Women love him and so will you, so you can relax.'

'Mal?'

'Short for Malik.'

'You're on intimate terms with a Crown Prince?'

'We were at college together. He'll be at the party, but you already know that because you've seen the guest list.'

'All the more reason why I'm the wrong person to take! I don't know any of these people and I will have no idea what to say to them. Please tell me he has a really friendly wife.'

'Not yet, and that is a very sore subject so I advise you not to mention it.'

'Why is it a sore subject? He's divorced? He wants a wife and he can't find someone to marry him?'

'He's rich, so it goes without saying that there are plenty of contenders. There was someone, but—' Lucas broke off, knowing that there was no one less qualified to comment on relationships than him. 'Never mind. Let's just say that for Mal duty comes before personal choice. It comes with the territory, I believe.'

'So he won't marry for love?' Her innocent question would have made him smile had the circumstances been different.

'No. Which will probably ensure the success of the union.'

She tilted her head as she studied him. 'When I get my T-shirt made, I'm getting you a matching one that says "Don't tell me you love me" on it. I can tell you now that I won't be any use at this party, not just because I'm not glamorous but because I know nothing about the politics of Zubran. What if I say the wrong thing?'

Every other woman he knew would have died

before admitting to feeling out of their depth socially.

'You won't say the wrong thing. And if you do—' he shrugged, fighting the desire to take her straight back to bed and lose himself again in her soft warmth '—I know him well enough to have you bailed from a jail cell.'

Her shoulders slumped in a gesture of defeat. 'I'll have to call my sister.' Her expression suggested that wasn't something she relished. 'Angie has Jamie all week and she relies on me at weekends so that she can go out. She'll be really annoyed if I tell her I can't make it.'

'And yet you're the one who slogs all week to provide the money for the family—' He caught her frown and bit off the rest of the sentence. What did he know about a functioning family? Absolutely nothing so he wasn't in a position to offer advice or opinion. 'Tell her you'll be back for Wednesday with a big fat bonus. The truth is you wouldn't have been driving there today, anyway. The roads around the castle are impassable and we are always low priority for the snowplough and the gritting lorries.'

'Can't you get them cleared?' Her innocent

faith in the breadth of his power and influence almost made him smile.

'I can have the estate cleared, but there are five miles of country lanes between us and the main road. I can work miracles, but local government bureaucracy requires more than that.'

'So if we're snowed in, how do you propose getting us to Zubran?'

'We're flying. We'll take the helicopter to the airport and then the private jet.' Relying on a well developed instinct that told him exactly when to push and when to retreat, Lucas strode towards the stairs without giving her the opportunity to argue further. 'Call your sister and then meet me downstairs in the kitchen. I'll make us breakfast.'

'Fine, I'll ring,' she muttered, 'but she's going to kill me. As long as you don't mind having that on your conscience.'

Lucas chose not to remind her that he didn't have a conscience.

It was a difficult phone call, not least because for the first time in her life she wasn't being honest with her sister.

'You stayed overnight with your boss? Are you *crazy*? Haven't you listened to a single word I've said to you over the years?' Angela's tone was sharp and Emma felt colour flood into her cheeks as she contemplated her sister's reaction if she were to find out the truth.

'I didn't have any choice. Have you looked out of the window? It's like the Arctic. The roads here are impassable.' There was no point in trying to explain that she'd been worried about her boss. That concern and care had kept her here long after she should have left. There was no way Angela would understand that. Nor was she going to understand the next part of the conversation. Bracing herself, Emma tightened her grip on the phone. 'Angie, do you remember the project I told you about? The Zubran Ferrara Resort that is opening next week?'

'Of course. It's all over the news. They're calling it an iconic structure and your boss is apparently a progressive genius much loved by eco nuts everywhere. They're missing out the fact that he cares more about buildings than people. Remember that, Emma.' Her sister's tone was sharp. 'The man is a heartless womanizer, incapable of sustaining a relationship.'

Not incapable. Unwilling. He'd been hurt so badly he didn't want to risk it again.

And he was obviously concerned that she was about to declare undying love. That she might start spinning one night into a lifetime.

Her sister was still talking. 'So what time do you think you'll be home?'

'That's why I'm phoning—' Emma closed her eyes and blurted it out. 'I have to fly out with him to Zubran, just for a few days,' she added quickly, 'and I'll be back for Jamie's play. I'm sorry. I know the timing is bad and there are things you're supposed to go to, but I'll make it up to you.' She was prepared for it and when it came it was spectacular.

'No! You can't do this to me! I have the staff party tonight!'

'I know, and I've already thought of that. I'm going to phone Claire and ask if she'll come and sit with Jamie so that you can go out. Why not? She was my best friend at school and she loves Jamie and he loves her.' Emma's heart was pounding. She hated fighting with her sister. Hated it. 'I'm sorry, Angie, I know it's really inconvenient but it's just a few days. Lucas needs me.'

'Before last night you were coming home for the whole week. And now, suddenly, he needs you? Just what form is this "need" taking? What the hell do you think you're doing, Emma?'

'My job. I'm doing my job.'

'Really? You're sure this is just about work?'

'Of course.' She couldn't allow herself to think it could be anything else. 'I know what you're thinking, and you're wrong.'

'Lucas Jackson is rich, good-looking and single. Are you seriously telling me you haven't ever looked at him like *that*?'

'He's my boss.' And he hadn't always been single, had he? There had been a woman who had meant something to him and they'd had a child together. A child they'd lost. His aversion to commitment wasn't the attitude of a mindless playboy, but a man who had shut himself off from emotion. Realising that her sister was waiting for her response, Emma forced herself to stop speculating. He'd made it clear that he didn't want to talk about it, so that was the end of that. 'Stop worrying about me. I'm sorry about the weekend, but it can't be helped.'

'No, of course it can't. You absolutely have to go to this urgent and very glamorous party while I'm stuck with Jamie.'

'Don't say that!' This time it was Emma who raised her voice. 'Do *not* say that you're "stuck with him". He might hear you and it would upset him so much. I know you don't mean that.'

'Maybe I do mean that. It's all right for you—you're living this amazing life in London and I'm stuck at home with a child who isn't even mine.'

Used to her sister's outbursts, Emma took a deep breath and tried again to work out if there was any way she could have Jamie living with her in London. The economics just didn't work. Her job paid well but it was demanding and required her to spend long hours at the office. And on top of that she wouldn't have wanted Jamie living in her area.

'We'll talk about this when I'm home. And I'll get Claire to take him so that you can go to your party tonight. And please, Angie, just go and give him a hug.'

'He's going through a horrible phase at the moment. I don't feel like hugging him.'

Emma bit back a response that she knew wouldn't be helpful in the long run. Angie loved Jamie, she knew she did, but her sister bitterly resented the impact that taking care of their brother had had on their lives. Swiftly she changed the subject. 'Have you picked out a dress for your party tonight?'

'I'm wearing the red one from last Christmas.' Angela sounded marginally less angry and Emma relaxed slightly.

'The one with the lace? You look lovely in that. I hope you meet someone gorgeous.'

'And even if I did, we both know he'd run a mile once he discovered that I come with a permanently attached nine-year-old brother,' Angela snapped. 'And talking of which, I have to go and make him breakfast. And on that subject, thanks for starting a routine of making pancakes on Saturdays because now I'm going to be glued to the stove for hours.'

'It doesn't take hours, and it's fun. We make them together. Jamie makes the mixture, I cook them.'

'He makes a mess when he cooks. It doubles the work. And talking of work, I'd better go and break the news that the good sister isn't coming home.'

'I'm not the good sister.' Emma thought that if Angela had seen what she'd been up to on the rug the night before, she definitely wouldn't have used that term. 'You're good too. It's just that you're tired and disappointed that I won't be able to take up the reins for a few days and that's understandable.'

'Stop being so bloody reasonable.'

Emma bit her lip. 'I'll be back on Tuesday. Have fun at the party tonight.'

There was a long pause and then Angela sighed. 'I'm sorry,' she mumbled. 'I'm a horrible bitch.'

Yes, Emma thought, you sometimes are. 'It's the end of term and you're just tired. And I promise that once I'm home you can just put your feet up and have some time to yourself.'

'So what are you wearing to this fancy party?'

'I've no idea. I suppose I'll have to buy something.'

'Just tell me you're not having dreams of being Cinderella.'

Emma looked around the turret bedroom, with its four-poster bed and velvet drapes. Then she looked at the rug in front of the log fire where, for a few special hours, she'd felt like the most irresistible, desirable woman on the planet. No one's sister, no one's PA and no one's stand-in mother. A woman. She closed her eyes and pushed the thought away. 'Can I speak to Jamie?'

'He's in the shower. He's going to Sam's to play this morning. I guessed it would take you a while to get home and I didn't want him standing by the window watching for you all morning and nagging me. From the sound of it it's just as well I made that decision.'

Emma felt a stab of guilt but at the same time she was relieved Jamie wasn't there to hear Angela's tirade. 'Tell him I love him and I'll call him again later.'

'If you're not too distracted by partying. Do I need to remind you that office romances never cause anything but trouble?'

'No, you don't need to remind me of that.'

'If you lose your job—'

'I won't lose my job.' Emma ended the call, depressed by the encounter. She knew what was behind it. She understood why Angela behaved the way she did and she didn't blame her for that, given everything that had happened in their family, but it was still hard to deal with.

She couldn't think of anything worse than losing the job she had with Lucas but nor could she imagine anything more uncomfortable than spending the next few days in his company after what had happened.

What she really needed was space to sort her head out.

She needed to persuade him to let her go. How was she going to do that? What was the one thing that would make Lucas Jackson send a woman as far away from him as possible? The answer came to her almost immediately and Emma gave a tiny smile. Yes, she thought. *That.*

CHAPTER SIX

EMMA went in search of Lucas, trying to shake off the guilt that shadowed almost every conversation with her sister. She found him downstairs in a kitchen that looked like something that would have featured in a magazine shoot for a perfect country home. In fact the whole place would make the most incredible family home, she thought, as she looked around her. It should have been filled with happy children and noisy dogs.

Had he originally bought it for that purpose?

Her mind buzzed with questions but they were all too personal and she was trying to make their relationship less personal, so she didn't voice them. And anyway, she knew he wouldn't have answered them. That one devastating revelation of the night before had been dragged from him purely because she'd held precious evidence in her hand.

As she walked into the room he glanced towards her and she saw in an instant that everything about his body language was guarded.

Exploiting that, she leaned against the doorframe and gave him a soppy look. 'While I was upstairs I was thinking a lot about last night.' Watching, she saw the tension ripple through him like a current ready to repel intruders.

'What about last night?'

'I know you don't want to hear this but—I think I love you, Lucas.' She blurted the words out, wondering if she'd injected just a little too much Scarlet O'Hara into her tone. 'Completely, totally, with my whole heart. For ever. I was saving myself for my perfect man and now I realise that man is you.' Intercepting his appalled glance she almost laughed. 'I know you don't want to hear it. It's *awful* that I feel this way and the truth is that I feel more strongly about you with every minute that passes. I don't know what to do! The longer I stay here, the more in love with you I am. Goodness knows what I'll be like by Tuesday. I suspect I won't be able to get through an hour without hugging and kissing you at every opportunity. I may even have to burst into a really important meeting just to get my Lucas fix. I'm so glad you're taking me with you.'

His eyes narrowed to two dangerous slits and then the tension left him. 'Nice try, but I still want you with me in Zubran.'

'But I *love* you. Madly. Passionately.'

'It doesn't matter how much you "love me",' he drawled. 'I won't be sending you home until the job is done.'

Emma slumped onto the nearest chair. 'You know you're unreasonable, don't you?'

'Demanding, yes. Unreasonable, no.'

Demanding.

He'd been demanding when he'd virtually dropped her onto the rug and stripped her naked.

He'd been demanding when he'd helped himself to her body.

She shivered and tried desperately hard not to think about that. 'Do you realise that when a woman says "I love you" you go white and then look as if you're about to go for dental surgery? Apart from hearing that the Dow-Jones has plunged a million points, I'm guessing that the worst words you can hear are "I love you" so

I'm going to be saying it every five minutes until I drive you so mad you'll leave me at home.'

'You have a warped sense of humour.' The sleeves of his sweater were pushed back and her gaze lingered on those strong arms, remembering the way he'd held her as the passion had ripped through both of them.

Emma squeezed her eyes shut.

This was impossible. Totally impossible.

'Coffee?'

She opened her eyes and stared into his. Blue now, but they'd appeared almost black last night in the firelight as he'd kissed her. 'Thanks.' Taking the mug from him she wondered whether she was going to be thinking about sex every second of every day for the rest of her life.

'So what did your sister say?'

'Oh, she was totally thrilled that I won't be able to make it home for the holiday—' Emma sipped her coffee, still feeling a bit sick at the thought of the conversation. 'She said something along the lines of, "Super, I didn't really want to go out and have fun anyway, so you just have a great time and don't worry about me".'

A wry smile touched his mouth. 'So she didn't take it well then.'

Emma tried not to look at that mouth. 'No. But I've messed up her weekend so I don't really blame her. She relies on me to take over from Friday night.'

'So she heaped on the guilt and you took it. Surely there are other options. Other relatives? Babysitters?'

'No relatives, just us. And we've never really used babysitters. I only see Jamie at weekends so I don't want to arrive home only to go out again.'

'Are those your words or hers?'

Emma put her mug down slowly, thinking that he was remarkably astute for someone who claimed not to care about people. 'Hers. But I think she's right.' Angie had Jamie all week. It would have felt wrong to go home and then announce she was going out on a Saturday night, wouldn't it? 'She was supposed to be going to a party tonight so I've texted my friend to see if she can look after Jamie but it's not something I've done before and it does make me feel bad.'

'So during the week you run around after me

and at weekends you run around after Jamie and your sister. What about your own needs?'

Emma stared at him. 'I love my family.' Truthfully she didn't feel comfortable talking about her sister. The whole conversation was still too raw and her guilt too fresh and it felt disloyal to talk about her family to someone who couldn't possibly understand. She knew he was judging Angie and she didn't want that because she knew the whole thing had been harder for her sister than it had been for her.

'Does your sister always make you feel guilty?'

'It isn't her fault. Family stuff is always complicated—you know how that is.' It was a casual comment. The sort of comment that might invite an understanding laugh from another person. But not him. And her own smile faded because she realised she had no idea whether this man even had a family. She knew so little about him. Just that he'd had a daughter. The photo had been of two people—a little girl and her daddy. No third person. Which didn't mean anything, of course, because the third person could easily have been behind the camera, but she found herself wondering who had taken the picture. Someone he loved? A passing stranger?

Suddenly cold, Emma stood up and walked towards the big range cooker that dominated the kitchen. If she'd been asked to design her perfect kitchen, this would have been it. Perhaps she would have added some soft touches, some cut flowers in the bright blue jug that sat on the windowsill, and a stack of shiny fresh fruit to the large bowl that graced the centre of that table, but they were just small things. She could imagine Jamie doing his homework on the scrubbed kitchen table while she rolled out pastry and made a pie for supper. She could imagine lighting candles for a romantic dinner.

She could imagine Lucas, dark and dangerous, sprawled in a chair while he told her about his day.

'Do you like it? My kitchen?' His tone was rough and she glanced up at him, shaken by her own thoughts.

'Just planning what I'll do when I move in.' Walking back to the table, she shifted the conversation away from the dangerous topic of family and onto something lighter. 'Add a few feminine touches here and there—flowers, china covered in pink hearts. And of course I'll tell you I love you every other minute until you get used to it.' The coffee was delicious. And strong. As she sat down, she felt the caffeine kick her brain into gear. 'So do you always look like you're about to have root canal work when someone says "I love you"?'

'I've no idea. No one has said it to me before.'

'What, never?' Genuinely shocked, Emma thumped her coffee down on the table. 'All the women you've been out with and not one of them has ever said it? Why?'

'Because I would have dumped them instantly. I don't pick the "I love you" type.'

So what about his daughter? *Had she not come from love?* The questions rolled around in her head but she stayed silent and sipped her coffee, grateful for the warmth and the fact that sliding her hands around the mug gave her something to do apart from try desperately hard not to look at him. She wasn't used to having indecent thoughts about her boss.

Emma lowered the mug slowly, knowing that she wasn't being entirely honest with herself.

Was she really going to pretend that she hadn't always found him attractive? Because that wouldn't be true, would it? Right from the beginning she'd found him scarily attractive, but the fact that she worked for him had put him off-limits. That and the fact that not once in the two years she'd worked for him had he given the slightest hint that the attraction might be mutual.

But that had all changed, hadn't it? And it was the shift to the personal that made it so awkward to be around him. Maybe it would have been different had there been other people here, but alone it felt—intimate. And yet they were still strangers. Intimate strangers.

She couldn't undo what had been done. She knew things now that she hadn't known before and there was no way of unknowing them. She knew he'd had a daughter and that he'd loved her. She knew he blamed himself. *She knew he was hurting.*

He said that he didn't have a heart but she knew that wasn't true. He had a heart, but that heart had been badly damaged. He was obviously suffering deeply but even without hearing the details, she was sure that he was wrong in his belief that he was somehow responsible for his daughter's death. That couldn't be the case.

'Emma?'

She gave a start. 'Sorry?'

'I asked if you were hungry.' Apparently suffering none of her emotional agonies, he pulled open the door of a large modern fridge and she found herself staring at his shoulders, watching the flex of male muscle under the black sweater. His body was strong and athletic and she felt the heat spread through her body, the flare of attraction so fierce that she almost caught her breath.

'Hungry would be an understatement,' she murmured. 'I'm starving. Right now I could eat ten camels. Which I suppose I might have to if you insist on making me go with you to Zubran.'

'I was thinking of omelette.' He turned his head and their eyes met. Tension throbbed between them, a living breathing force, and she stood up on legs that shook and threatened to let her down.

'I love omelette. Where will I find a bowl?'

'You think I need your help to cook a few eggs?'

'Sorry. Instinct.' She sat down again, relieved

to take the weight off legs that seemed to have forgotten their purpose. 'I usually do the cooking when I'm home. I'm teaching Jamie to cook—it's one of the things we do together. Every Saturday we make pancakes for breakfast, it gives us time to talk. And then we pick a different dish. Last week we did pizza. Today we were going to make Christmas cake—' She knew she was talking too much but she couldn't help it. She talked to fill the silence because otherwise she found it too disturbing. 'Of course, because of you, we won't be making Christmas cake but you don't need to feel guilty about that.'

'I won't.' He pulled a box of eggs out of the fridge while she watched.

He'd showered but he hadn't shaved and his jaw was darkened by stubble that made him look more bandit than businessman. She remembered the roughness of it against her skin, the heat of his mouth, the touch of his fingers—

She remembered all of it.

She closed her eyes. This was not working. Forget love—all she wanted was to be able to be in the same room as him and not feel this almost unbearable sizzle. She wanted to be able to listen to what he was saying without thinking of everything else that he could do with his mouth.

She wanted to be able to look at him without thinking of sex.

She wasn't sure whether the fact that he clearly wasn't suffering the same degree of torment made it worse or better.

Better, she told herself firmly. Definitely better. At least one of them was still sane.

And then she caught his eye briefly, caught a glimpse of darkness and heat, and knew that she was wrong. He was feeling everything she was feeling. He was fighting everything she was fighting.

The knowledge made her limbs shake and she clutched her mug, her heart banging against her ribs. 'So tell me about this place. It's not somewhere I would have expected you to own. You're all about glass and cutting-edge design and this must have been built by Henry the Eighth.' She was chattering frantically to cover up the way she was feeling but of course he knew exactly what was going on in her head.

And he wasn't going to do anything about it.

His self-discipline in all things was legendary.

Except for last night.

Last night, he'd lost control.

But there was no sign of that now as he glanced at the walls of the kitchen. 'Slightly earlier than Henry the Eighth, with later additions. And it's true that if I'm designing a new building then I like to make use of modern techniques and materials, but that doesn't mean I don't love old buildings. The history of this place is fascinating. And I don't own it by myself.' He broke eggs into a bowl and whisked them expertly. 'When it came onto the market, Mal, Cristiano and I bought it. It's owned by a company we set up together.'

'Mal, the Prince? And Cristiano Ferrara who owns the hotel group?'

'That's right.' He poured eggs into the skillet and they sizzled in the heat. 'The plan is that once I've finished the restoration, we turn it into an exclusive hotel that will probably be rented as a whole. We're planning to hold traditional British house parties.'

'I love that idea.' She'd known he had powerful friends but it wasn't until today that she'd realised just how powerful. 'I didn't even know this sort of place ever came up for sale. How did you find out about it?'

He tilted the pan. 'I'd had my eye on it for a while.'

'Who owned it before? It must have been awful to have to sell something like this.'

The change in him was visible and immediate. That beautiful mouth hardened into a thin, dangerous line that made her immediately conscious that she'd somehow said the wrong thing.

'It was built by a wealthy merchant in the thirteen-hundreds,' he said evenly, 'and stayed in the family until the last member gambled away all his money.'

'Gambled? Horses?'

'Much more twenty-first century than horses.' Lucas tilted the pan slightly. 'Online poker.'

'Oh. How awful.' She glanced round the kitchen and tried to imagine owning something like this and then losing it. 'Imagine losing something that had been in your family for centuries. Poor man.'

'That "poor man" was a selfish, miserable excuse for a human being who took great pleasure in using his wealth and status to bully others, so don't waste your pity on him because he certainly doesn't deserve it. More coffee?'

Emma was so astonished she couldn't answer. It was the first time she'd ever heard him make an emotional comment about a business deal. 'You work with plenty of wealthy, selfish human beings. Who was this guy?'

Lucas slid the omelette onto her plate, his expression blank. 'He was my father. You didn't give me an answer about the coffee so I'll just top it up anyway, shall I?'

Had he really just said what she'd thought he said? 'Your *father*?'

'That's right. My mother was his archivist. She left university and found her dream job here, working with the collection that had been pretty much neglected. She worked here for fifteen years and they had an affair. But he wanted to marry someone with the right heritage and apparently that wasn't my mother—' his tone was flat '—so she lost a job that she adored, her home and the man she loved. Not that she should have worried too much about the last bit. I think that could have been considered her lucky break, but obviously that's just my personal opinion. Unfortunately, she didn't see it that way.'

It was the most he'd ever told her about himself. The first really personal exchange they'd had. 'So she basically had an affair with the boss.' Emma felt her mouth dry and he looked at her with that keen, perceptive gaze she found so unsettling.

'If you're making the connection you appear to be making then I can assure you there are no similarities at all. This was a lengthy relationship which was supposedly based on love and trust—' his tone was threaded with cynicism '—whereas—'

'You don't need to finish that sentence.' She interrupted him hastily. 'We've been over this a thousand times already. I know what last night was.'

'Do you?' He was unnervingly direct and she knew that there was no way she could confess that she couldn't stop thinking about it. Still less could she admit that it wasn't just the sex she was thinking about; it was *him*. The more she discovered about him, the more her vision of him shifted. He was no longer her cold, detached boss. He was a man with a past.

'I love my job. I'd never do anything to jeopardize that. To be honest I can't *afford* to let anything jeopardize that. And I'm not in a position to have a relationship with anyone right now. There isn't room in my life. And then there's the fact that you're far too bitter and twisted for me.'

He frowned slightly, those dark brows pulled together in silent contemplation as if he wanted to say something else. And she didn't want him to say it. She wanted him to stop talking because every time he spoke he revealed something else and the more he revealed the more personal it became.

'So your mum discovered that she was pregnant, and then what?' Colour touched her cheeks as she remembered a small detail from the night before. The man had been half out of his mind with drink and grief, but he hadn't forgotten the condom, as if some part of him was programmed to remember. And she was relieved about that, of course, because the situation was already complicated enough without adding to it, but still, it made her wonder.

'He duly announced he was getting married to another woman. Perhaps if she hadn't made that fatal mistake, he might have let her stay. He was perfectly happy to have a lover on the scene, but a child would have made the whole thing vastly inconvenient and not at all British, so that changed things.' The words flowed from him and it was so unusual to hear him talk like this that she sat still and just listened. She wondered if he even realised how much he was telling her.

'So your mother resigned?'

'No. My mother never would have resigned so he had to find another way of getting rid of her.' He sat down across from her and picked up his fork. 'He accused her of theft. So not only did he humiliate her and ruin her chances of getting another job, but he made her hate him. And it made her hate me too, because I was inadvertently the reason for all that.'

The lump in her throat came from nowhere. 'Couldn't she have taken him to court or something? Got some help?'

'I don't know what went through her head. Maybe she did talk to a lawyer. I don't know, but certainly nothing came of it—' he sliced his omelette in two '—all I know is that it was a struggle. We lived in the smallest room you have ever seen. It had just one window and it never let in enough light.' He frowned. 'I couldn't work out why anyone would have designed a window that didn't do the job it was intended to do. That was when I started to dream about buildings. Buildings with space that let in the light. I drew myself a house and promised myself that one day I was going to build it and live in it.'

It was easy to imagine him as the child, drawing his dream. Especially when you saw the man he'd become. 'Did he never acknowledge you?'

'No. And the irony was, he never had any more children. I was his only child. Now isn't that poetic justice? He wanted a family. The tragedy was that he actually had one, but he never acknowledged it. You're not eating. Is there something wrong with your omelette?'

She'd been so lost in his story she hadn't taken a single mouthful of her food. 'Did you meet him?'

'When she found out that he had no living heir, my mother was determined that I should have the recognition that she felt was my right.' His mouth twisted. 'Or maybe she was hoping that he'd take me on so that she could have her life back.'

'You went to see him?'

'Yes, but not because I wanted him to suddenly play "Dad". I wanted to give him a piece of my mind. And his response was that it didn't matter what she did, he would never give me Chigworth Castle. I was thirteen years old and so angry with him that I punched him, then I told him he didn't need to give it to me because I was going to just take it from him when I was ready. It gave him quite a laugh, this skinny kid without a penny to his name trying to give him a black eye and then threatening to take his castle.' He gave a cool smile. 'He wasn't laughing on the day I took ownership. Cristiano Ferrara fronted the deal so he had no idea who was buying it until it was sold. Not that it would have made any difference. He'd spent all his money so he wasn't in a position to negotiate or withdraw. But I wouldn't have put it past him to burn the place to the ground rather than stop me owning it.'

There was a dull ache behind her ribs. 'When was this?'

'Eight years ago. I was twenty-six, my career was on the rise and I'd landed a few huge commissions that proved to be life-changing.'

'The art gallery in Rome.'

He lifted an eyebrow. 'You've been reading my biography?'

'I work for you,' she reminded him. 'I send your biography to the media and prospective clients on a daily basis.' And with that single unthinking sentence she reminded him of the true nature of their relationship. The atmosphere shifted instantly.

'Of course you do,' he said smoothly, 'and that is why I want you with me in Zubran. Because you know all these things.' Once again he was cool and distant as he pulled out his phone and checked an email. 'I've been waiting to hear from Dan.'

Dan was his pilot and Emma often spoke to him about Lucas's travel arrangements. 'Is the airport even open?'

'Yes. They've cleared the runway and there is no more snow forecast so we shouldn't have any trouble with our flight.' He scrolled down, checking his other emails. 'The helicopter will pick us up from here in an hour. I assume you have your passport with you?'

The shift from personal to professional was startling but she went along with it. What was surprising was not that he'd suddenly stopped telling her about his past, but that he'd ever told her in the first place. He'd given her another glimpse of a private, secret part of himself. And she was gradually building up a picture of a very different man from the one the public saw.

She knew so much more about him than she had yesterday. And she suspected he would rather that wasn't the case.

She was going to forget it, she vowed, and just get on with the job. That would be best for everyone.

'I have my passport, of course.' There had been many occasions when she'd flown with him on short business trips to Europe and a few times to the US. She'd enjoyed the variety and as long as the trip hadn't eaten into her precious weekends, she'd never objected. 'The one thing

I don't have is clothes. And I assume there isn't time for me to go home and pack.'

'No. We have to leave immediately and anyway, the roads are impassable. You're fine for the journey.' His eyes lingered on her sweater then lifted to her face. 'You can travel in what you're wearing and you can go shopping tomorrow before the meeting.'

'I have to wait until tomorrow?'

'Seven-hour flight, four-hour time difference—' he shrugged '—it will be evening when we arrive and you're already exhausted which is hardly surprising given the amount of sleep you didn't get last night.'

Presumably she wasn't supposed to react to that. Presumably she was expected to treat what had happened with the same matter of fact casualness as he did.

So that was what she did. 'Is there somewhere to shop close by?'

'Avery will be able to advise you on the best place.'

'Avery owns her own highly successful company.' Emma thought about the pictures she'd seen of the glamorous businesswoman. 'She's very nice and we've bonded over your guest list, but I suspect she and I may have a very different idea of what constitutes the "best" place.' It was all too easy to imagine how her sister would react if she blew a sizeable chunk of her precious salary on a dress she'd probably only ever be able to wear once in her life.

'I'm paying,' Lucas drawled, 'so the budget is irrelevant.'

'You most certainly are not paying.' Emma shot to her feet, deeply offended that he could even think she would agree to that. 'Just in case you hadn't already noticed, I am *not* Tara.'

'Let me stop you there before you embarrass yourself,' he interjected softly, leaning back in his chair and stretching out his legs, as supremely relaxed as she was ridiculously tense. 'I am offering to buy you clothes because you don't have any with you and because I'm asking you to dress for an event you're required to attend in your role as my PA, *not* because we had sex. I am in no way being contradictory. I am completely clear about the nature of our relationship, Emma. It's professional.'

And for a moment she'd forgotten that. And he

knew she'd forgotten it. Feeling intensely foolish, Emma sat down again. And this was the
problem, she thought helplessly. For her, the personal and the professional were now well and
truly mixed up. It was impossible to separate
them. When he'd mentioned buying her clothes,
she'd assumed it was personal. 'Well, thanks
for clearing that up, but I don't need you to buy
me clothes for work either. I can buy my own
clothes.'

He watched her steadily, a cynical gleam in
his blue eyes as he acknowledged her tension
and the reason for it. And along with the cynicism there was a tiredness that came, not from
lack of sleep but from life. 'Right now, I think
whether or not I buy you a dress is the least of
our problems, don't you?'

He thought she couldn't do this.

Determined to prove him wrong, Emma lifted
her chin and stood up. 'I don't have any problems. Do you?'

Zubran was an oil-rich state on the Persian Gulf.
She'd expected sand. What she hadn't expected
was the fascinating mix of red-gold sand dunes,

mountains and stunning coastline that she saw from the air as they came in to land. The scenery provided a welcome distraction from dwelling on the change in her relationship with Lucas.

And really, there was nothing to think about. She worked for him. If she wanted to carry on working for him, she had to pull herself together.

It helped that, from the moment they'd boarded the company jet, he'd been very much his old self. As focused as ever, he'd worked for the entire flight, pausing only to drink one cup of strong black coffee while, seated across from him on one of the ridiculously luxurious deep leather seats, Emma fretted and worried.

It was just a couple of days, she told herself. A couple of days during which she had to behave in a professional way and switch off any other thoughts. After that, once they were back in the office, everything would be easier.

'Fasten your seat belt,' he murmured, 'we're landing.'

She wondered how he knew that, given that he hadn't even looked up from his work. 'I know. I've been looking at the scenery. I expected desert.'

'Zubran is famous for its coastline. The country has a long seafaring heritage and the diving here is incredible which is why I incorporated an underwater theme in the design of the hotel.'

Emma watched as a graceful catamaran danced over the waves beneath them as they came in to land. 'How far is the hotel from the airport?'

'Half an hour along the coast. The Ferraras never build hotels in cities. They're all about fresh air and healthy living.' Finally he glanced up, but only to exchange a few words with the flight attendants who had found themselves seriously underutilized on this particular flight.

As soon as they landed, he was out of his seat, impatient to get on. 'Let's go and see if my hotel is still standing.'

The short walk from the aircraft to the sleek limousine waiting for them on the tarmac was enough to tell her that a shopping trip needed to be high on her list of priorities. The sweater that had provided woefully inadequate protection against a British winter now felt as thick and heavy as a fur coat. She was grateful for the fierce air conditioning that turned the interior of the car into the equivalent of a mobile fridge as they sped along a straight road that led from the city up the coast. Rising to her left were steep sand dunes, turning from gold to red under the warm glow of the late afternoon sun, and to her right were the warm waters of the Indian Ocean, sparkling like a thousand tiny jewels thrown onto a carpet of blue velvet.

The change in climate felt surreal after the howling winds and thick snow of England.

Knowing that the moment she stepped out of the car she was going to melt, Emma glanced at her watch. 'What time do the shops close? I need to buy something to wear that isn't made of wool.'

'You don't have time to shop tonight. I've asked Avery to put something in your room for this evening and she's going to take you shopping in the morning. After the meeting you should have time for a short rest.'

'A rest? Am I three years old?'

'No, but tomorrow is going to be a long night.'

'I don't need a rest to prepare for that. I will run on adrenaline.' Emma felt a tiny thrill of excitement. Was it a bit sad, she wondered, to be this excited about a party that was supposed to be business? She was supposed to be saying to herself, *What a bore, working when I'm supposed to be on holiday.* Instead she was thinking, *Yay, a party.* She was feminine enough to enjoy being given the opportunity to dress up and mingle with adults. And anyway, this wasn't any party. It was *the* party. People had been virtually clawing each other out of the way to get on the guest list.

Lost in thought, she hadn't even noticed that they were no longer on the main road until she looked up and there, ahead of her, rising up as if from the sea itself, was a beautiful glass structure in the shape of a shell. Of course she'd seen both the plans and the model, but nothing prepared her for the real thing.

'Oh.'

'All that hard work and your only response is "oh"? Let's hope my audience tomorrow night are a little more enthusiastic.' Smiling faintly, Lucas unclipped his seat belt as the car pulled up outside the main entrance.

Emma was so busy staring she stumbled as she left the car. 'I said "oh" because I was lost for words, not because I wasn't enthusiastic, not that I think for a moment my approval means anything to someone like you.'

'Perhaps it does.' He spoke softly and she turned her head to look at him, her heart beating hard. Warmth engulfed her and she repeated the word in her head like a mantra—*professional, professional.*

'In that case you should know that I think it's stunning. Beautiful and very clever. It must be hard designing something that works for this climate.'

'Despite the fact we're on the edge of the desert, it can become surprisingly chilly at night, although not as chilly as a castle in snowy Oxfordshire.' A frown on his face, he removed his gaze from her mouth. 'Air circulation and humidity was a challenge, as was the soil type but in the end it's all come together.'

The heat was starting to make her feel strange and she didn't know whether it was from the ferocious desert sun or the heat that came from being close to Lucas.

They reached the entrance and were greeted by a beautiful girl dressed in a smart uniform.

'Mr Jackson. Welcome! I hope your journey

was comfortable.' She shook hands and then glanced at Emma, clearly expecting to see Tara. A consummate professional, her smile didn't slip. 'Welcome to the Zubran Ferrara Spa Resort. I'm Aliana, Head of Guest Relations. I hope your stay is comfortable, but if there is anything at all you need then do please ask.'

And judging from the woman's expression, nothing was off-limits, Emma thought, feeling a rush of jealousy that she knew was totally inappropriate.

'This is Emma,' Lucas said calmly. 'Emma is my PA.'

'Of course.' Despite the smooth response it was obvious that the girl considered 'PA' to be a euphemism for a very different role. 'If you follow me, we have your suite ready. And Mr Ferrara asked me to pass on a message when you checked in.'

'Message?'

The woman cleared her throat. 'The message was, "Tell him he's in the Presidential Suite and if it leaks I'm never working with him again." His words,' she said hastily. 'I'm just the messenger. I'm absolutely sure that nothing you designed would ever leak, Mr Jackson.'

Lucas simply laughed and Emma was about to ask why there would be any concern about the Presidential Suite leaking when a pair of glass doors in front of them opened with a smooth hiss and they walked down a gentle slope and into the most breathtakingly beautiful room she'd ever seen.

'We're under the water. Oh my—' she gasped as a shoal of brightly coloured fish swam right in front of her, darting through softly floating fronds of seaweed. 'It's amazing. Like being inside an aquarium.' For some reason she hadn't noticed this on the model. Or maybe she had, but just hadn't registered that it would be under the water. She was always so busy, she realised, she never really had a chance to appreciate the scope of his genius. It was truly imaginative. And restful.

'It's not entirely under the water. Just this room.' Frowning, Lucas turned to the woman. 'I told Cristiano to use the suite.'

'Mr Ferrara is here with his whole family, including his young daughters,' the woman said.

'His security team decided that the Coral Suite is more suitable for small children because it's possible to close off the pool. And you are, after all, the guest of honour. This amazing, iconic hotel is your brainchild.' She looked suitably star-struck but if Lucas even noticed, there was no sign of it.

'Right.' He put his briefcase down on the table. 'And when is the Prince arriving?'

'His Royal Highness sends his apologies. He intended to join you for dinner tonight but instead he finds himself tied up with a delegation from Al Rafid. He looks forward to joining you at the party. As you know, every royal and celebrity in the world has been holding their breath hoping for a ticket.' Smiling, she handed him a slender object that looked like a remote control. 'The technology in the hotel is quite staggering but I suppose I don't need to give you a lesson on that, given that you were involved in all stages of the planning. It's all voice controlled.'

Voice controlled?

Emma had been so busy gawping that she was barely listening. She'd never been anywhere so luxurious. The use of glass made it feel as if they were actually on the water, part of the sea rather than the land. And it had been furnished to reflect the same sea, soft leather sofas designed for lounging, the floor covered in rugs in marine shades of blue and turquoise.

As the woman left them alone, she glanced around her. 'Voice controlled? So exactly which part of it is voice controlled?'

Lucas was prowling around the suite, checking various details. 'Everything. The lights. The blinds on the windows. The sound system. You can operate it all without once moving from the bed.'

His choice of words made her flush but fortunately he wasn't looking at her.

'So if I say music—' She stopped, enchanted as the smooth notes of Chopin flowed through the room. 'Oh that is *so* cool.'

Lucas observed her delight with a lifted eyebrow. 'That is just the default track. List the track you want and it will play it. And you adjust the volume by saying "volume up" and "volume down". I wish I could install something similar in my clients,' he drawled. 'And now you need to get dressed. I'm taking you to dinner.'

It was the last thing she'd expected him to say.

Ever since she'd woken this morning he'd been careful to keep his distance. He'd warned her off. Apart from that one unguarded confession in the kitchen, their relationship had reverted back to employer and employee. During the journey he'd been cold and more than a little intimidating.

But now he wanted to take her to dinner, in this beautifully romantic place where the sun was just setting?

She should say no. Her heart raced away in a frantic rhythm. 'I don't have anything to wear.'

His eyes were on his phone as he checked his emails. 'Avery has just sent a message to confirm that she arranged for a selection of clothes to be delivered to your room. She'll pick you up at ten tomorrow to shop for something to wear at the party.'

'But—'

'Whatever she's picked out should hopefully be enough to get you through until the morning.'

But Emma wasn't thinking about the dress. She was thinking about having dinner with him. She was wondering why he'd changed his mind.

'Lucas—' Her voice was croaky. 'Is this a good idea? Do you really want to have dinner?'

'Of course.' He didn't glance up from his emails. 'The restaurant is the most complex part of this structure. I want to see whether the end result gives the dining experience that I hoped for when I designed it.'

Dining experience?

Emma stood still, horrified to realise how close she'd come to making a total fool of herself yet again. Once again, her brain had twisted his words. A week ago if he'd mentioned dinner she would have assumed it was all about business. Now, she was imagining soft words and the promise of something more, whereas the reality was that when he'd asked her to have dinner with him it hadn't been a romantic proposition, but a practical one. It wasn't that he wanted to have dinner with *her*. It was that he wanted to have dinner in the restaurant he'd designed, and she was supposed to accompany him.

She breathed deeply, hating the fact that she felt disappointed. And as for the hollow feeling inside her—well, she hated that too.

Registering her prolonged silence, he finally glanced up. 'Is something wrong?'

'Nothing. I'll just go and change.'

Enough, she thought as she walked quickly into the second bedroom.

Enough.

How much clearer could he make it? Where was her pride and her common sense? From now on she was going to think of him as her boss and nothing else. That way, she not only got to keep her job, she got to keep her sanity.

CHAPTER SEVEN

THE situation was a thousand times more delicate to handle than he'd anticipated. He'd seen her face when he'd invited her to dinner and knew instantly that he'd made a major miscalculation. She'd wanted dinner to be something else. Despite all his warnings, she'd hoped. And he, who shattered women's hopes on a regular basis without thought or care, had found it hard to shatter hers. But shatter them he had and she'd slipped quietly away to the second bedroom with her dignity intact and had been there ever since.

Cursing softly, Lucas dragged his hand over the back of his neck and wondered if she'd been crying. The thought disturbed him far more than he would have expected.

He checked his watch again. Should he knock on the door and check on her? Avery Scott was nothing if not ruthlessly efficient so he doubted that the problem was with the clothes. Something she'd provided was bound to fit, surely? So what was taking her so long?

Reluctant to become embroiled in an emotional conversation that could only make the situation between them even worse, he decided to give her another few minutes.

Restless, he paced through to the living room and switched on the news headlines. If nothing else it would provide him with dinner conversation.

'I'm ready.' Her voice came from behind him, crisp and businesslike and he turned, relieved that she sounded like the Emma he knew but then he saw her and realised that this woman was nothing like that Emma.

His instruction to Avery had been to provide clothes. He hadn't bothered to spell out the fact that those clothes should be practical rather than seductive. He'd seen dinner as an opportunity to talk business, agree the schedule of media interviews and all the other details they had to discuss and had assumed she'd dress accordingly. He'd expected a sober, sensible outfit in muted colours. Instead, he was greeted by a tempting swirl of vivid scarlet that was neither muted nor sober.

The dress flowed rather than clung, the cut and quality of the fabric skimming her curves. Curves that he remembered with disturbing clarity. Curves that sent him from a state of relative calm to one of intense arousal.

Knowing that he was in trouble, Lucas breathed deeply. 'I'm sorry. I hadn't realised she'd pick something so—' he fished for the right word '—red. You must be furious.' *He* was furious. And he wondered for a moment whether Avery had done it on purpose. It wouldn't have been the first time she'd tried to match him up with someone.

'You don't like it?'

'It's not exactly…practical.'

'Well, we're just sitting eating dinner, so how practical does it have to be?' Apparently oblivious to his struggle, Emma stroked her hands over her hips. 'It's not at all what I would have chosen, which is half the fun if I'm honest. It was clever of her to find something at short notice. I have no idea how she knew my size—' Her eyes narrowed as she looked at him. 'Ah.

You must have told her.' And if she were embarrassed about that, then there was no sign of it.

Lucas ground his teeth. Wasn't she supposed to be blushing and shy or something? Instead she seemed aware of her femininity in a way she hadn't been only days earlier. Or maybe he was the one who was suddenly aware of it. Watching her hands stroke her hips made him think of the way she'd touched him and suddenly he wanted to get her out of the damn dress and into the silk sheets of his bed. But if there was anything more dangerous than sleeping with this woman once it would be sleeping with her twice.

'If you don't feel comfortable wearing that to dinner then I can ask the hotel to send something else.'

'What would be the point of that? And I don't want to risk offending Avery when I'm finally about to meet her in person. I know I've only ever spoken to her on the phone but we get on really well.' She closed her hand around a slim purse. 'It's just a dress, Lucas. I hardly think a dress is going to bother you if it doesn't bother me.'

It bothered him.

It seriously bothered him but he couldn't tell her that without taking the conversation into areas he was determined to avoid. Given that fact, he had no choice but to accept the fact that the red dress was her chosen outfit for the evening.

The tension in him mounted. 'If you're too tired to join me for dinner I quite understand.'

'Tired? Don't be silly. I can't wait to see the restaurant. I remember it on the model and the plans and I'm so excited. I can't remember when I last went out to dinner. I mean, I know this is work,' she added, throwing his own rule right back at him, 'but I'm ridiculously excited to eat something I haven't had to cook myself.' Her enthusiasm was genuine and charming but he didn't want to be charmed. The feeling unsettled him in a way that was new to him.

Deciding that keeping his hands off her might well turn out to be the biggest challenge of his life, Lucas gestured to the door of the suite. 'In that case we should go. We have a table reserved. Can you even walk in those shoes?' They were clearly designed for sex, not walking. Before last night he would never have been able to imagine

Emma in shoes like that, but now they formed an erotic addition to those incredible legs.

'Of course I can. I've been practising in my room. That's why I was late. Watch me.' Grinning, she walked up to him, a look of triumph on her face. 'See? I don't even wobble. It's all to do with putting your weight on the right part of your foot.'

She was different, he thought. Her skin glowed, her eyes shone, she *sparkled*.

And then she lost her balance on those heels and tumbled against him. With lightning reflexes, Lucas caught her. His hands closed over her shoulders, his fingers biting into warm flesh. Just that simple touch took him back to the night before and suddenly he wanted all of it again. Her lips, her warmth, *her incredible body.*

His mouth was dangerously close to hers and he was dangerously close to doing something about that. Furious with himself for being so weak-willed, he gave a growl of frustration and was about to pull away when she calmly detached herself.

'Oops. Sorry about that. Clearly your first assessment was right. I need more practice in the shoes.' Not looking at him, she tightened her grip on her purse. 'Shall we go? We don't want to be late.' And, with that, she walked towards the door, the wicked red dress swirling around her gorgeous legs.

Dropping two phones into her bag, Avery Scott kicked off her shoes and curled up on the soft sofa in the private dressing room of the exclusive boutique. 'You'll have to excuse me, but I've done enough of these parties to know that I'll have blisters by ten o'clock if I don't rest now. This is my last chance to sit down so I'm taking it. So—spill. While we're waiting for them to bring clothes, tell me all.'

'Do you seriously have time for this?' Trying to ease the pain in her feet, Emma flopped down next to her, thinking how nice it was to have female company. Her life was so frantic she'd let her friendships slip. Apart from the occasional exchange at the water cooler, she rarely chatted with anyone. 'Those shoes were gorgeous but it was a bit like walking round with my feet in the jaws of a crocodile. It's really kind of you to help me shop, but don't you have a million other things you should be doing before tonight?'

'I employ good people and I delegate. Now forget the shoes and tell me how that red dress looked.'

'It looked great. Too great. Lucas acted as if I'd chosen it on purpose to try and seduce him, which was pretty unfair given that I had nothing to do with it.'

'So did you? Seduce him, I mean.'

'No, of course not.'

'Ah.' Avery's beautiful eyes sparkled. 'Want to talk about it?'

'No. Let's just say that tonight I'm wearing a grey sack.' She was joking about it, but inside it didn't feel funny. It felt hopeless. It didn't matter what she did, things between them were never going to be the same again. They couldn't undo what they'd done. 'I work for him and I really need the job and now I've…I've messed it up.'

'How have you messed it up?'

Emma rubbed her fingers over her aching head. 'It's not really something I should even be talking about. Just make sure I pick out a boring dress so that I blend into the background tonight.'

Avery shuddered. 'I've never intentionally picked a "boring dress" in my life. I'm not sure I could even if I tried and I don't intend to try. Tell me what is going on.'

Emma was surprised by how badly she wanted to confide. 'You don't need to hear my problems.'

'Yes, I do. I'm fantastic with other people's problems. It's just my own I can't solve. And you're not the first woman to sleep with her boss.'

Emma gave a groan but didn't bother denying it. 'It's such a cliché.' And before she could stop herself she was blurting it all out. Everything. From the loneliness of living alone in London in the week, to the row with her sister and sex on the rug. The only thing she didn't mention was Lucas's daughter or the fact that his father had never acknowledged him.

That information was private. His secret, not hers to tell.

'Wow.' Effortlessly elegant, Avery uncurled her legs and sat up. 'You've led this life driven by duty and responsibility and then suddenly on one snowy night it's all blown apart. That's *so* romantic.'

'It's not romantic. It's embarrassing and inconvenient. And my life hasn't been driven by duty.' Emma shifted uncomfortably. 'It isn't like that. I adore Jamie.'

'I never said you didn't adore him, but that doesn't change the fact you've always put him first. And you're so different from Lucas's usual type of woman.'

'What do you mean by that?'

'You're the home and hearth type that Lucas usually avoids like a non-alcoholic cocktail.' She gave a slow smile. 'And you spent the night together. How interesting.'

'It's not interesting. In fact I think it's fair to say he was appalled. He thought it meant I would automatically fall in love with him.'

'Whereas you were already in love with him.'

'No, absolutely not! I don't love him.'

'Probably why you slept with him,' Avery said helpfully, ignoring Emma's denial. 'Let's just hope he doesn't figure that one out. So—you've freaked him out. Lucas Jackson is Mr Cool so

I'm looking forward to meeting the freaked-out version.'

'He is *so* freaked out he spent all yesterday making sure I knew it was never going to happen again. And he was really angry about the whole thing.'

'Definitely freaked out,' Avery murmured, 'which would explain his reaction to the red dress.'

'No, that was just because he thought it was too frivolous for work.'

'You think so?' Avery gave a cat-like smile and pulled her phone out of her purse as it rang. 'Excuse me for one moment while I get this—'

While Avery solved some problem that involved lighting and fireworks, Emma brooded on the grim reality of her situation. She wasn't in love with him. It would be madness to fall in love with a man who would never love her back. Even greater madness to be in love with her *boss*.

After his initial response to the dress, Lucas had returned to his detached, slightly intimidating self. Their evening had been starchy and formal. Their whole relationship had changed.

They couldn't go backwards and it seemed they couldn't go forwards either.

'Right—where were we? Ah, the dress—' Avery came off the phone and looked at her. 'You were saying that he found it incredibly sexy.'

'I didn't say that. I said he was angry.'

'Presumably because he found you attractive and didn't want to.'

'I've no idea. I work for him and I want to carry on working for him. But I have to stop feeling this way.'

Avery shrugged. 'A man like Lucas Jackson comes along once in a lifetime. My advice? Take the sex and get a different job. Problem solved.'

Emma gaped at her. 'I could never pick sex over job security. You don't understand—'

'I'm the child of a single mother. A strong single mother, so believe me I do understand about the importance of job security. And I'm not really suggesting that you throw in a job just for sex, but it seems to me that this isn't the job for you anyway. You need to find something closer to home so that you can have a life. Maybe this is the trigger you need to make you do that. You've had far too much responsibility and not enough fun but we're going to fix that.'

A job closer to home? 'Even if I were prepared to look for another job it wouldn't make a difference. He isn't interested in a relationship. And I made a total fool of myself last night because when he invited me to dinner, just for a moment I thought he meant *dinner*, if you know what I mean.' She thumped her forehead with her fist and Avery looked amused.

'Yes, I know exactly what you mean. So the first thing you have to do is find out whether or not Lucas is interested. Wear a really knockout dress tonight.'

'He'll think I'm trying to seduce him.'

'Not if you don't try to seduce him. Wear the dress but be businesslike.' Avery narrowed her eyes. 'If you dance, you dance with other people. If you talk, you talk to other people. Any connection with him should be brief and businesslike. If he really doesn't want you then he'll be fine with that. If he does—well, we'll see.'

'No, we won't see! He's my boss. He pays well and he's a good employer.'

'I pay well and I'm a good employer. You could

always work for me and I don't care where you're based as long as the work gets done. Now let's get started on these clothes.'

Unable to summon up any enthusiasm, Emma slipped off her shoes. 'I thought after his reaction to the red, we'd better go for something a bit more muted. Maybe beige?'

'Sure. Let's just put you in a canvas sack and have done with it, shall we?' Avery shuddered. 'Emma, you are *never* wearing beige again. Your beige days are totally behind you. I've earmarked a nice boring navy dress for you to wear in your meetings this afternoon because it will make the contrast all the more startling when you dress up tonight, but your days of dressing like a nun are over. They're fetching me a selection of dresses and while we're waiting you can tell me something about Lucas, apart from the fact he rocked your world. What's going on behind that handsome face?'

'He's a clever man. Very talented. I'm really lucky to work for him.'

'I love a bit of moody, cerebral introspection as much as the next girl, but that isn't exactly what I was asking. I want to know why the man has never settled down. You do realise that of all the women he's ever been with, his longest relationship is with you?'

'I'm not a relationship. I'm his PA.'

'And before you he was getting through a PA every six weeks. But you've stayed the course. That has got to mean something.'

'It means I need the job too badly to resign.'

'Or that you've become important to him.'

Her heart skipped. 'Only in the sense that I make his work life run smoothly.'

'Really? So why did he bring you here?'

'Because he and Tara broke up and he needed someone with him.'

Avery gave a womanly smile. 'And you don't think Lucas Jackson has a million replacements waiting in the wings? Come on, Emma. He wanted *you*. And I'm so pleased he finally dumped that awful Tara.' She poured two glasses of water and handed one to Emma. 'Tara got horribly drunk at one of my parties a year ago and we had to tactfully remove her before she stripped on the dance floor. I've been wishing her bad karma ever since.' She frowned as the personal shopper in the exclusive store arrived with a selection of clothes. Within seconds she'd dismissed them all. 'I saw this bright blue dress at one of the shows in fashion week that would be perfect.' She named the designer and described it and the girl hurried off while Emma looked on in amazement.

'Do you know every dress in every designer's collection?'

'No. Only the ones that catch my eye. The others I forget—' Avery drank the water and looked longingly at the bowl of fresh dates that had been put on the table. 'I am starving, but if I eat that I'll never get into my dress for tonight. Ah—' She sprang to her feet as the girl returned carrying a sheath of midnight-blue silk. Avery took the dress from her with a crow of triumph. *This* is the one. I would have bought it myself if I hadn't already picked one out for the party. It's going to look perfect on you.'

'How much is it?'

Avery rolled her eyes. 'Who cares? Just try it on. Every woman should own at least one dress like this. It is going to turn you from a sensible, professional woman into a wanton sex goddess.'

'Firstly, Lucas wants sensible and professional

and secondly I'm not remotely wanton sex goddess material.'

'You will be by the time I've finished. Now shut up and try the dress, Emma. You're old before your time and we're going to fix that.' Avery thrust it at her and waved away the saleswoman with a winning smile. 'We're fine here. Thanks. But some more water would be great. That's another thing I have to do before a big party. Hydrate. Go and change, and while you're undressing tell me how you concentrate while you're working with Lucas. I'd be lying on his desk panting hopefully every morning saying "Take me, take me".'

Giggling, Emma slipped behind the curtain and slid her skirt off. 'You wouldn't really. He's horribly moody in the mornings. I try not to speak to him before he's had at least two cups of coffee.'

'I'm good with moody men. Are you dressed yet?'

'Nearly.' Surprised by how much chatting to Avery had lightened her mood, Emma slid the dress over her head. 'I think it might be a bit tight.'

The curtain was whisked back and Avery stared at her. 'Oh Lucas, Lucas,' she purred, 'you are in *so* much trouble. I almost feel sorry for you.'

Emma gave a nervous laugh. 'You don't think it's too tight?'

'That's not tight. It's called a perfect fit. Have you even looked in the mirror?'

'Not yet, but—'

'Then look.' Avery spun her round and Emma stared at her reflection.

'Oh my God.'

'Yes. My thoughts exactly. And the back of it is—'

'Non-existent.' Emma felt a lurch of excitement and terror. 'I don't look like me.'

'Yes, you do. But it's you as you've never seen yourself before.' Eyes narrowed, Avery reached forward and twisted Emma's hair into a loose knot. 'Hair up, hair down… Up, I think. Then he'll fantasize about letting it down over your beautiful, bare back.'

'I don't want him to fantasize about me! We're trying to get things back to normal, not make them worse! Avery, you have to stop this.' And she had to stop it too. She had to stop thinking about that night. She had to stop thinking of him as anything other than her boss. She had to—

Her eyes met Avery's in the mirror.

'The man is delicious and it's time he got together with someone decent instead of choosing shallow, brainless women who are only interested in his money and contacts. I'm going to arrange for you to have hair and make-up in your suite—' Avery whipped her phone out and sent a string of emails. 'Do you own any diamonds?'

'Of course not. Nor do I go anywhere that I could wear any.'

'Well, tonight you are. That dress needs diamonds,' Avery murmured without looking up. 'I'm going to arrange for one of the jewellery companies to loan you something for the evening. Smile—' She snapped a photograph with her phone and then proceeded to email it to someone. 'They will be able to decide what will look best with that colour and neckline.'

'OK, stop! Now you're going over the top.' Emma backed away. 'Tonight is about work. I'm supposed to be mingling and networking, not parading around in diamonds.'

'I've never understood why a woman can't look her best while she's mingling and networking,' Avery murmured. 'I suspect Lucas Jackson hasn't been so interested in a woman for a long time—maybe never. We should make the most of that.'

Emma found herself trapped. She couldn't tell Avery that the only reason Lucas had slept with her was to get through a truly terrible night. So now Avery had totally the wrong impression and this whole situation was spiralling horribly out of control and all she could do was mutter a lame, 'He's not interested.'

'He's interested. He noticed the red dress. Men only notice what a woman is wearing when it makes them think of sex.'

'Avery!'

'What?' She looked up from her phone. 'You are very, very pretty. You deserve diamonds.'

'I do not want to be wearing anything valuable. What if someone steals it from around my neck?'

'Do you want an estimate of the combined wealth of the people attending tonight?'

'No. I assume that the Crown Prince alone is worth a fortune. I wonder why he isn't married?'

Avery's smile faded and her pretty face lost some of its colour. 'Because, like you, he puts duty before his personal needs. Only in his case he intends to marry the boring virgin princess his father has picked out for him. I don't know who I feel more sorry for.'

'How do you know that?' Emma stared at her. 'Oh! You and he—'

'Yes. But not for a while.' Avery gave a bright smile. 'Our Sultan-to-be needs a well behaved obedient bride prepared to honour and obey and, as you've probably guessed, I am *so* not that person. Even if I could occasionally obey, which is a major struggle if I'm honest, I totally bombed out at the word "virgin".'

Emma wasn't fooled by the light tone. 'You're in love with him.'

'God, no,' Avery answered just a little too quickly. 'I'd never be stupid enough to love a man who doesn't like me to argue with him. I'd never be so stupid as to love a man, full stop. Now what are we going to do about shoes for you?'

Emma looked at her closely but Avery was back to normal again as she made arrangements for the dress to be delivered to the hotel.

'I'm worried this outfit is over the top. I'm his PA. I work for him and I want to continue working for him. This whole thing is so complicated.'

'Welcome to the real world. Love *is* complicated. Why do you think I'm so careful to avoid it? Nothing can ruin a perfectly planned and ordered life like love.'

'I'm not in love.' Horrified and defensive, Emma removed the dress carefully. 'Absolutely not.'

'So here's a little tip from an expert—' Avery's tone was conversational as she helped Emma out of the dress. 'If you don't want people to know you're in love, be careful not to let your face light up like a halogen light bulb when his name is mentioned. I'll deal with this while you get dressed—no, not the skirt you arrived in. Try this blue linen. It's cool and professional. Perfect for meetings.'

It was just physical attraction, Emma told herself as she slid into the blue dress. She *liked* him, of course she did, but she wasn't in love.

'How is the dress? Businesslike?'

'It's perfect. What about you? Has there been someone else since the Prince? You must meet gorgeous men all the time.'

'I do. Unfortunately I have a congenital urge to want what I can't have.' For a fleeting moment Avery's eyes were sad and then she shrugged. 'Are you ready?'

'But if you have feelings for him then this whole party must be hell for you, because the Prince is going to be here,' Emma said slowly as the implications sank in. 'Why didn't you turn it down?'

'Pride.' Avery gave a lopsided smile. 'If I turned it down, people would think I was broken-hearted and I don't want him to have that power over me. I intend to go out there and show that his careless, heartless attitude hasn't made a dent in me.'

But Emma could see that it had. A big dent. 'You must feel terrible.'

Avery gave a careless shrug. 'Nothing that a pair of killer heels won't cure. That and the money they'll be transferring into my account when I've given them a party that no one is going to forget. This is business, Emma. I never feel terrible when I'm parting the rich from their money.'

Emma felt a flash of admiration. 'You make me feel guilty for moaning. If you can go out there and pretend you're not bothered so will I. Just share the secret of how you do it.'

'Look fabulous,' Avery said simply. 'Show him what an excellent time you are having without him. And if it gets too much just text me and I'll meet you in the Ladies. We can both cry in the toilet.'

Seriously distracted, Lucas tried to concentrate as Cristiano Ferrara outlined his objectives for the proposed development in Sicily. Across from him sat Emma, making notes in her usual efficient manner. Her hair was twisted into a severe, businesslike style and today she'd chosen to wear sober navy. A perfect choice. He'd insisted that their relationship remained professional and she was following that instruction with the same efficiency with which she followed every other instruction.

Everything should have felt fine.

It didn't.

In the past he'd always managed to compartmentalize his life and Emma fell into the category marked 'work', but suddenly the edges of those compartments had broken down. Instead of focusing on the business, he found himself focusing on *her*. He noticed things he hadn't noticed before, like the way she listened attentively to everything that was being said. She never missed a thing, which was what made her so good at her job. He was used to mixing with women who continually monitored their appearance and the effect they were having on the men around them. Emma did neither. If she was even aware of how she looked, she gave no sign of it.

He, however, was all too aware of it.

Never before had he had trouble forgetting a woman but he was finding it impossible to forget his one night with her. And it wasn't just the physical, he thought. It was so much more than that. The fact that she'd stayed when she could have left. The fact that she'd refused to leave him even though she had responsibilities else-where. The way she'd tidied up all the evidence of the party so that he wouldn't be upset. *The way she'd covered him with a blanket.*

He wasn't used to being on the receiving end of anyone's warmth or compassion. He'd made his own way in the world, nurtured himself and provided his own comfort.

And now...

Just one night, he thought savagely. It had been just one night and he hadn't been able to con-centrate since. His body was in an almost per-manent state of sexual arousal and as for his mind...

'We'll do a site appraisal,' he said, realising that his friend was waiting for a response, 'and then come back to you with an outline design that incorporates the features you just described.' It had been a mistake to bring her to Zubran. He'd thought he would be able to continue as if nothing had happened, but that was proving more of a challenge than he'd anticipated.

Across the table, Cristiano raised an eyebrow in expectation. 'Any initial ideas? Concepts?

Normally, you're already sketching by this point in our discussions.'

Normally, his brain wasn't full of inappropriate thoughts. 'You want me to build in the shadow of the largest active volcano in Europe. We'll have to analyse the soil and consider the possible effects of volcanic activity. It isn't an ordinary project by any means. Naturally we'll address the usual issues of sustainability but air quality might have a negative impact on photovoltaic systems so we'll need to be creative in our design.' They talked at length about the Ferrara vision for the hotel while Emma continued to make notes.

Lucas knew that whatever emails needed to be sent would already be winging their way through cyberspace. She was as ruthlessly efficient as he was. Nothing went undone. Nothing was forgotten.

'Fly over soon.' Cristiano's tone was conversational. 'Why not spend a few days with us? Mix business with pleasure. I'll take you to see the site and you can get a better feel for the area.'

Mix business with pleasure.

He'd already done that, Lucas thought, with

devastating consequences. He'd thought it would be easy to put that one night behind him, the way he'd put other nights behind him in the past. But this time was different.

'Emma will put a time in the diary.'

Immediately she lifted her eyes and smiled acknowledgement, but the smile was for Cristiano, not him, and Lucas felt a flash of anger because she hadn't looked at him once during the meeting. Nor had she looked at him when she'd returned from her shopping trip with Avery. The fact that his reaction was illogical made no difference to the degree of his response. Nor did the fact that Cristiano was a happily married man and that Emma's smile had been friendly rather than flirtatious. There was nothing to explain the sudden surge of jealousy. It was a primitive response, entirely out of character for him and inappropriate given that the focus was an employee.

As they closed the meeting, Emma walked round the table to Cristiano and Lucas could hear her asking after his wife and children. He clenched his jaw as the Sicilian businessman withdrew his phone and showed Emma a series of photographs.

It was typical of Emma to know everything about everyone, he thought. It was what made her such an excellent PA. Nothing escaped her. She forgot nothing. She knew names, faces— hell, she knew whole family trees.

Angry with himself, Lucas rose to his feet. 'If we're finished then we need to move on.' He shot Cristiano a pointed look. 'You and I have a string of media interviews to get through today.'

Work, he thought. The answer was to bury himself in work as he'd always done in the past and hope that the dress Emma had chosen to wear tonight was less provocative than last night's choice.

He could only hope that her sudden interest in navy would extend to evening wear.

CHAPTER EIGHT

EMMA stayed in her room until the last minute, rehearsing her expression in the mirror. Cool. Composed. Not bothered.

True to her word, Avery had arranged for both a hairdresser and a make-up artist to come to the suite so she'd been pampered and spoiled while Lucas had been tied up giving interviews to the media. She hoped that his mood would have improved. During the meeting he'd looked ready to explode.

A brisk knock on the door made her jump. 'Emma?' Lucas's voice came through the door. 'A security team has just delivered a necklace for you. Are you ready?'

Yes, she was ready. Or as ready as she'd ever be.

Pride, she reminded herself, thinking of Avery.

Breathing deeply, she opened the door. The white dinner jacket was a shock. She'd expected black and the dramatic contrast between the white and that raven hair made her hold her breath and not release it for a long moment. He was effortlessly elegant, everything masculine and altogether unobtainable. Despite all her best intentions, her stomach tied itself in a knot and of course he had to see her reaction because he was a man who saw everything. To calm herself, she focused her attention on the box in his hand. 'I hope it's nothing over the top. Avery arranged it. She thought the dress needed something.'

His gaze scanned her in a single sure sweep. No doubt he'd done the same to countless women far more beautiful than her but still she couldn't look away from him, this man who had been told he was nothing and had made himself something.

She'd expected at least a polite smile, but he wasn't smiling. Instead his expression was deadly serious and when he lifted those dangerous blue eyes to hers she felt suddenly dizzy.

The situation called for a light, jokey response but there was nothing like that in her head so Emma simply held out her hand for the dark blue velvet box. 'Can I see?'

When he didn't hand it over, she reached and took the box from him, knowing that if she wanted to keep her job she had to prove to him that she could do this. That she could be every bit as detached as he was.

He probably thought she was dressing for him. She had to prove she was dressing for herself.

'I feel uncomfortable wearing anything valuable.' She discovered it was possible to speak as long as the subject wasn't personal. Flipping open the box, she gave a gasp. 'Oh it's gorgeous.' It was a sapphire pendant and her heart gave a little skip as she imagined how it might have felt to be given such a gift by a man who loved her.

Killing those thoughts fast, she was about to lift it from the case when Lucas did it for her.

'Turn around,' he said roughly and she turned without thinking and then heard his sharply indrawn breath and remembered that the dress swooped low on her back.

Would he say something?

There was a pause. A moment when she held her breath and willed that admirable restraint of his to splinter. She closed her eyes and waited, wanting desperately for him to just grasp her and take control as he had that night in the turret bedroom. She wanted all of that urgency, all of that wild passion, and then felt guilty because she knew that urgency and passion had been fed by raw emotion and a situation so painful that no one would want to repeat it.

And then she did feel his hands on her skin, cool and steady as he fastened the necklace. The touch was minimal, but even that was enough to set her alight. Even with her back to him the attraction was so fierce that it took her breath away and she was relieved he couldn't see her face because she was sure everything she felt would be visible. No make-up, however clever, could conceal feelings so powerful. And now she had to pretend that their relationship hadn't changed even though it had changed beyond recognition.

'The meeting seemed to go well.' She couldn't say any of the things she wanted to say so she talked about work. 'It's the first time I've met Cristiano in person, although I've talked to him on the phone a lot. He's not as scary as his reputation.'

'He liked you.' There was an edge to his tone

that she didn't understand and she picked up her wrap and then turned, smiling, making sure that nothing of what she was feeling inside showed on the outside.

'I'm ready if you are.'

From the moment they set foot out of the hotel it was clear that this was going to be a party like no other. Flames shot into the air from torches, and what appeared to be a million tiny lights lit the paths that wound through the grounds towards a spectacular marquee large enough to accommodate hundreds of people. Emma felt a rush of excitement because she'd never, ever in her life been to an event like this one.

'It's incredible,' she breathed and Lucas glanced down at her, registering her delight with a frown that made her wonder what she'd done to annoy him.

'Avery Scott is very good at her job.'

'Good? I'm not good, I'm brilliant.' A sultry female voice came from behind them and Emma watched as Lucas's mouth curved into a smile. And that smile made Emma catch her breath. To describe him as handsome would be to do him an injustice, she thought, watching as a passing waitress dressed as a mermaid slid a tall, slender-stemmed glass into his hand.

'Avery—' he leaned forward and kissed the cool blonde on both cheeks '—you've surpassed yourself. It's spectacular. Thank you.'

'My pleasure. May you both have an absolutely brilliant and unforgettable time and don't forget to tell your friends, as long as they're rich and can afford me.' Avery extracted herself from Lucas without smudging her lipstick and winked at Emma. 'I am *loving* that dress. Lucas, what do you think? Am I a genius or am I just incredibly good at what I do?'

Lucas gave her a speculative look. 'Be careful.'

Avery chose to ignore the warning. 'She is nothing like your usual type. Hang onto her.' She gave him a friendly punch on the arm and Lucas gave a slight frown.

'She's the best PA I've ever had so I certainly intend to.'

Avery was scanning the crowd, looking for problems. 'That wasn't what I meant, and you know it, you utterly infuriating man. Now go and enjoy the party.'

'Emma doesn't like parties.'

'Emma doesn't go to parties,' Avery said gently, 'which isn't the same thing at all. She's going to totally love this one because I organised it and it's going to be perfect.'

Emma never found out how Lucas would have responded to that because at that moment there was a clacking sound in the sky and Lucas glanced over his shoulder towards the beach where a helicopter was landing. 'Looks as if the Prince has arrived.'

The change in Avery was instantaneous. All the fizz and bubble went out of her, like a glass of champagne that had been left sitting overnight on a table. 'If you'll excuse me, duty calls. I expect I'll see you both later. Have fun.' Without looking in the direction of the helicopter, she walked away on heels that should have made it impossible to balance. Emma, who could guess how bad she was probably feeling, wondered if she should follow.

'She and Mal have history,' Lucas drawled, 'but don't mention it now because here he comes and it isn't a good idea to talk about Mal's past relationships. Unless Cristiano and I are teasing him in private, of course. Smile. He's royalty.'

The next few minutes were a blur of introductions.

Emma found the Prince seriously intimidating. Surrounded by heavyweight security, he dominated his surroundings, which probably wasn't surprising given his status. What was surprising was the fact that he didn't dominate Lucas. The two men stood side by side, equal in height, stature but also achievement.

They talked easily, as old friends and peers, and as she listened, Emma realised that it was Lucas she was listening to, not the Prince. It was Lucas she was looking at. She hungered to feel that beautiful mouth on hers, to feel those hands on her, to dig her fingers into the luxuriant blue-black hair.

In despair, she looked away. *She was completely obsessed about a man she couldn't have.*

Was this how Avery felt all the time?

Emma sneaked a glance at the Prince, still in conversation with Lucas, and wondered if the feeling was one-sided. Was Avery also in love with a man who couldn't love her back? There was no sign of an inner struggle on that bronzed, handsome face. No hint that tonight might be as difficult for him as it was for her.

And then she saw the moment the Prince picked out Avery in the crowd and saw him go utterly still as the woman who loved him so deeply turned her head to look at him. Their eyes met and held.

Knowing that she was witnessing a private moment that shouldn't be witnessed, Emma turned away quickly feeling a flash of deep empathy with the other woman. And also for Mal because in her own small way she understood about responsibility and duty.

And then she felt guilty even thinking that because although it was true that she had a responsibility towards Jamie, he was also her brother and she adored him.

And if she had put her own life on hold, that was her fault, wasn't it? Not Jamie's. He'd never asked her to do that.

But Angie had. *I've had him all week and now he's yours.*

Emma frowned as she realised how much she'd allowed her sister's attitude to affect her. How much she'd tried to compensate for Angie's lack of warmth towards their brother. Angie expected her to take responsibility at weekends and Emma had gone along with that because she adored spending time with Jamie and because—she breathed deeply—and because she was afraid to stand up to her sister.

Jamie wouldn't care if she occasionally booked a babysitter and went out. But Angie would. Angie would ladle on the guilt.

She straightened her shoulders.

That had to change. And she had to be the one to change it.

She was standing here now, wearing a dress that made her feel incredible, because someone else had pressured her into it but she realised that she could have done this by herself if she'd made the effort. Not the party and the illustrious company—of course not that—but dressing up and meeting new people. She could have done more of that. She *would* do more of that. This holiday, she was going to sit her sister down and tell her that things needed to change for all of them.

And then Lucas drew her to his side and the next moment he was introducing her to someone and she was smiling, and talking, and making bright conversation even though the only coherent thought her brain could produce was *I want him*. They mingled, met what felt like a million people and Emma kept smiling until she felt her face would crack, until her cheek muscles were tired and her head throbbed with the effort of making polite conversation. She shook so many hands and kissed so many cheeks that faces and greetings blurred.

It seemed that everyone wanted a piece of him and she noticed people bunching close by, all waiting for the chance to talk to Lucas Jackson.

And then finally they moved towards the marquee, the magnificent tent lined in swathes of midnight-blue silk, studded with glittering jewels that shone like a million tiny stars in a night sky and the music slid into her and suddenly she wanted to dance and dance. She wanted to make up for all the times in her life she hadn't danced and she turned to Lucas, eyes glowing.

'Is it allowed? Can we?'

He narrowed his eyes as if he sensed the change in her but didn't quite understand it. 'It's allowed, but I don't dance.'

Emma was about to argue and persuade him

when he turned to speak to yet another acquaintance—*did he know everyone?*—and she reminded herself that she could dance without him. That dancing without him might actually be a good thing. She was allowed to dance and have fun and the music was fast and infectious so she just walked away from him and onto the dance floor feeling ridiculously free. She never did this, did she? She so rarely did something just for her, because she wanted to. Sex, she thought as she closed her eyes and let the music take her. That was something she'd done just because she'd wanted to. Because it had felt right at the time, just as this did.

And now she danced because she couldn't *not* dance with the music washing over her and the smiles of the people around her. And she was smiling too as she raised her arms like everyone else and threw her head back and let her body move to the rhythm.

'Good to see you letting your hair down.' It was Carlo, the Ferraras' cool, enigmatic lawyer who she'd been introduced to at the meeting earlier in the day.

And she danced and worked hard to have

fun, ignoring the small nagging part of her that wanted to be dancing with Lucas.

Dancing was personal.

It was a good job he'd refused her.

He'd brought this on himself.

He was the one who had insisted she join him at the party. He was the one who had sent her off shopping to buy something suitable so he had no one to blame but himself if she returned with a dress that made him think nothing but indecent thoughts.

He'd refused to dance with her because he knew it would make a difficult situation even more difficult and the result of that was that she'd danced anyway, and now she was with Carlo, the Ferraras' smooth-talking, handsome lawyer and it required a superhuman effort not to stride through the crowd of dancers and drag her away from him.

Did it make it better or worse that she wasn't even looking at him?

Better, he decided and then thought that no, actually, it probably made it worse.

He told himself that she was just dancing,

as were about a hundred other people around her, but then the music slowed and she slid into Carlo's arms, the change in the tempo of the music immediately altering the atmosphere. The dancing shifted from impersonal to personal. Lucas watched through narrowed eyes as Carlo's hand curved into the centre of Emma's back. That smooth, bare back that had been distracting him all evening.

Lucas had a sudden image of firelight on soft skin and suddenly he was striding across the dance floor, through entwined couples, until he reached his target. If he'd been asked to explain his behaviour he couldn't have done so. Never before had he cared enough to extract a woman from the arms of another man but he did it now without pause or hesitation.

'My dance.' It was a command, not a question and Carlo acknowledged that with the lift of an eyebrow, but he clearly saw something in Lucas's face because he reluctantly released Emma.

'Perhaps I'll see you later,' he murmured and Lucas felt his mood grow darker by the minute.

'She'll be busy later. But thank you for looking after her while I was busy with clients.'

Emma's eyes widened and she opened her mouth to speak, but Lucas slid his arms around her and moulded her against him before she could object. For a moment she stood stiff and he thought she might push him away. Then she sank against him and he held her the way Carlo had held her, except that this was an entirely different intimacy because their bodies already knew each other. That recognition was there and with it the memories and he felt the shiver pass through her and into him. It was no longer just a dance.

They were surrounded by people and yet they might as well have been alone for all the difference it made to the attraction.

As Carlo strolled away from them, Emma looked up at him. 'You were rude.'

'You asked me to dance.'

'That was earlier. And you said no.'

'So? I changed my mind.'

'In the middle of a dance? You couldn't have waited?'

No, he couldn't have waited and the knowledge unsettled him because impulse and urgency had no place in his life and he didn't want to feel this way. *Never had felt this way before.* 'He was be-having in an inappropriate manner.'

'We were just dancing. What's inappropriate about that?'

The image of Carlo's hand on her bare back was burned into his brain. 'For someone who supposedly loathes parties you appear to be hav-ing an incredible time.'

'I *am* having an incredible time. And I never said I loathed parties. Just that I never have the chance to go to any. I'm making the most of it and enjoying myself. I would have thought you'd be pleased.'

'Why would I be pleased?'

She sighed. 'Not *pleased* perhaps, but I didn't think—' She hesitated, staring at his shirt and not his face. 'I thought this was what you wanted. I didn't really think you'd care what I did in my own time.'

It was a reasonable, logical comment but noth-ing about the way he felt was reasonable or logi-cal.

Aware that people were watching them curi-ously, Lucas closed his hand around her wrist. 'Let's get out of here.'

She didn't argue and he felt her pulse flutter against his fingers as he strode off the dance floor virtually towing her behind him.

'Could you slow down? I'm still an amateur at walking in heels.' She tugged at her wrist but he didn't let her go until they were out of the crowd and back outside under the starry sky.

Then he released her and she stared at him, confused by what was going on and he had no answer for her unspoken question because he was confused too. And he wasn't used to feeling confused. *He was never confused.*

'Do you think it's unprofessional of me to dance? Is that what's wrong?' She spoke slowly, clearly ticking off possible explanations in her head. 'I did ask you and I thought as we'd done the meeting and greeting it would be—'

'It wasn't unprofessional.'

'Then—'

'Just drop it, Emma.'

'How can I drop it? You've dragged me off the dance floor so I've obviously upset you in some way. You have been glaring at me since you gave me that necklace. And in the meeting this afternoon you were glowering.' Her fingers fiddled with the jewel at her throat. 'I understand that you regret what happened the other night, but as far as I'm concerned it's in the past. Honestly, you don't have to worry. It's true that I wasn't sure I'd be able to get back to how we were, but I've discovered that I can. I know I can.'

Then she was doing better than he was because he didn't know that at all. 'So were you dancing with Carlo because you wanted to or because you wanted to prove to me that what we shared hasn't affected our relationship?'

'Does it even matter?' She looked back towards the tent, leaving him with only a glimpse of her profile and the curve of her dark eyelashes.

'You should be careful around Carlo.'

'Oh for goodness' sake, Lucas—he's the Ferraras' lawyer. I've spoken to him a few times on the phone when he's called the office and he is a really nice guy.'

'Based on what evidence? Because he's good-looking? Because he's charming? You're not exactly an experienced judge given the number of relationships you've had in your life.'

This time she looked at him with eyes that

questioned his sanity. 'Carlo grew up with the Ferrara brothers. They are lifelong friends, so presumably they see admirable qualities in him. I suppose the way we feel about people is coloured by our own experience. Perhaps you're too harsh a judge and no one would blame you for that given your background.'

'Perhaps you're naïve.'

'I was dancing with him, not proclaiming undying love. Don't you think you might be overreacting?'

Overreacting? Lucas dragged his hand over the back of his neck. 'Maybe I can read his mind better than you can. He's a red-blooded male.'

'Even if you're right about that, why would it matter to you? You've made it clear that you want our relationship to stay professional and nothing else so actually it's irrelevant. You don't have to watch out for me. That isn't your role.' She paused as a couple walked past them, arm in arm, and then lowered her voice. 'We agreed not to talk about this and we certainly shouldn't be talking about it here.'

'Good point. So let's go somewhere we won't be disturbed.' Knowing that he was acting irrationally, Lucas closed his hand around her wrist again and drew her along the path towards the hotel, walking so fast she almost stumbled.

'For goodness' sake, Lucas, you can't just leave! There are people hovering waiting to talk to you.'

'I don't care.'

'You are not making this easy.'

'I don't care about that either.'

'Where are we going?'

'Somewhere private. Somewhere we can talk without an audience.'

She'd never seen him like this before. They were at a side entrance to the hotel and, barely pausing, Lucas swiped a card through a scanner and the doors opened.

And Emma saw immediately that they were back in the Presidential Suite but this time via a private entrance that led straight onto the beach.

The doors purred closed behind them and she waited for him to release her but instead he kept his fingers locked firmly around her wrist as he strode into the living room.

She wondered if she ought to point out that

he was breaking his own rule. 'Lucas, we really ought to—'

'Maybe you'll push him too far, have you thought of that?' His tone was raw and savage. 'Maybe he seems like a decent human being until circumstances turn him into something else.'

Emma blinked, confused, and then realised that he was no longer talking about Carlo, he was talking about himself. About what had happened between them two nights before and her breathing jammed because she'd been trying so hard *not* to think about it. 'Lucas—'

'And when that happens, maybe you won't spot the signals, because you didn't spot them with me, did you? You didn't know when to back off. You could have left. You should have left. But you didn't. And then—you couldn't stop me, could you?' His tone was thickened and the breath caught in her throat because she could see that he was on the edge and she'd had no idea that his feelings were so intense. *She'd thought it was just her.*

'I could have stopped you. But I didn't want to.'

'Why? Because you're such a giving person you were willing to sleep with me to help me out?'

'No. Because I find you incredibly sexy and always have. Yes, I could have left, but I didn't want to. I *chose* not to. I could have stopped you but I chose not to do that either. And I'm glad I didn't because what we shared was special to me. Not just special—' she paused, wondering how honest to be '—it was the most exciting, erotic experience of my life. I don't regret it. I would do exactly the same again.'

'Would you?' His eyes met hers and suddenly it was hard to breathe.

'Yes.'

There was a brief pause and then they moved towards each other at the same time. Her arms were round his neck, his hands in her hair, their mouths hungry for each other as they kissed.

His mouth on hers, Lucas groaned deep in his throat. 'I promised myself that I wasn't going to do this again.'

'Then I'm so glad you're breaking your promise.'

He lifted his head but his hand remained

locked in her hair as if he couldn't quite bring himself to let her go. 'It's wrong of me. Selfish.'

'No—' Standing on tiptoe and lifting her face to his, she breathed the word against his lips. 'It can't be selfish if I want it too, and I do want it, Lucas. I want *you*.' Bold now, she traced his lips with her tongue and he gave up the fight, cupped her face and kissed her back, taking everything she was offering and demanding more. And the kiss was everything she remembered. He kissed with skill and assurance but this time she was determined that he should know this was her choice. That *he* was her choice. So she placed her hand in the centre of his chest and pushed him off balance. He fell back onto the bed and before he had a chance to recover Emma straddled him, pinning his arms above his head, smiling at his stunned expression.

'Forty-eight hours ago you were a blushing, shy, inexperienced woman.'

'So? I have a lot of time to make up for. Now be quiet and kiss me the way you kissed me the other night—' She brushed her mouth over his and he captured her face in her hands before sliding his hands down her bare back.

'The dress is beautiful but it has to come off.'

Smiling, she released his hands and sat up, carefully drawing the dress over her head. 'Seems a shame to take it off.'

'It's not a shame from where I'm lying.'

The dress slid in a slippery heap to the floor and suddenly she was back in his arms and his mouth was hungry on hers. Her hands tore at his clothes, impatiently stripping away jacket and shirt until he was naked too, until there was nothing between them except feelings and the truth. His eyes were fierce but she knew hers would be too because she wanted this every bit as much as he did. Perhaps she'd always wanted it, from the moment she'd walked into his office on that first day and seen him lounging behind his desk, remote and untouchable.

This time it was slow, where last time it had been fast. Everything stretched out, the intensity of it as agonizing as the anticipation.

Her mouth roamed over him and she heard his breathing change and felt powerful and desirable as she discovered how her touch affected him, how the stroke of her hands could drive him wild, how the flick of her tongue had him reaching for her. And he let her explore, until finally he could stand it no longer and closed his hands over her hips, shifting her above him in a sure movement that brought her into contact with the heat of his arousal.

Emma held her breath as she took him into her, felt the power and the fullness and then there was nothing but the rhythm and the incredible need that consumed both of them as they surrendered to it. Still holding her, he drove himself deep and she groaned his name against his lips, holding back the words that she so desperately wanted to say, knowing that honesty would ruin the moment. None of that mattered. Nothing mattered. Not the future nor the past, just the present and she gave in to that and allowed it to take her until they hit the same peak. They kissed their way through it, sharing all of it until she thought she'd die from the pleasure.

Lucas lay still, holding her, wondering why he had no desire to just get up and leave as he usually did.

'What was her name?' Her voice was soft in the darkness and what surprised him wasn't the question, which he understood immediately, but the fact that he wanted to answer.

'Elizabeth. I named her after my father's mother. Her great-grandmother. I liked to think that had she still been alive perhaps she would have done the decent thing and recognised her granddaughter. Either way, I wanted Elizabeth to know who she was and be proud of it.'

'I like that. He refused to acknowledge you but you created the link anyway.' Her arms tightened around him as she showed her approval. 'It's a pretty name.' There was a moment's silence and then she held him tighter. 'I know you don't want to talk about your daughter, but whatever happened I know it wasn't your fault. You are so wrong to blame yourself.'

'You're making that judgement without knowing the facts.'

'I may not know the facts, but I know *you*. I know it wasn't your fault. I know you would have done whatever could have been done.'

Lucas stared into the darkness. 'Your faith in me is touching but misplaced. I was a lousy father, Emma.'

'That isn't true. And I should know because I

had one. Or rather, I didn't have one. The man who fathered me wasn't interested in that role. He walked out after my sister was born. He came back soon after and my mother once told me that the reason she had me was to try and bring them closer together. How she could ever have thought a man who had never wanted one child would have been suddenly happy to have a second, I have no idea. He walked out for the final time while Mum was in the hospital with me. I've never even met him.'

Suddenly he understood more clearly why she would have avoided relationships. She had no reason to trust men. And she shouldn't be trusting *him*. Knowing that this was going to end badly, he tightened his grip on her. 'That must have been tough.'

'It was, but tougher for my mum and my sister. My sister especially because she always felt that for him to walk out there must have been something lacking in her. Which was wrong, of course. There was something lacking in him, but that isn't true of you so don't ever tell me again that you were a bad father.'

'I didn't leave, but I might as well have done.'

And suddenly, wrapped in her warmth, the words that had been jammed inside him for years flowed. 'It was snowing. Exactly like the other night. I'd been working long hours, trying to juggle several big projects. Because I often worked late and Elizabeth would be asleep by the time I arrived home, I was the one who got her up in the morning. We had breakfast together. That was our time together and it was always just the two of us because Vicky never emerged before eleven. That morning we had breakfast as usual. Nothing was different. You have no idea how many times I have gone over and over it in my mind, trying to work out if I missed something, but I don't remember anything out of the ordinary. I made her toast. And I cut her toast into the shape of a house because I always did that.'

'She must have loved that.'

'She did. She always ate the chimney first. I kissed her goodbye and promised her I'd take her to the park in the morning. Then I dropped her at school.' Remembering it was agonizing, the desire to put the clock back and do things differently almost overpowering. 'I left a note for

Vicky telling her I'd be home before she had to leave for the party.'

'You weren't going to the party with her?'

'I wasn't interested in spending an evening at a party where I knew no one. I wanted to be with my daughter. I was planning to leave the office at five to give me plenty of time to get home. Just before I left I had a phone call from Elizabeth's teacher, wondering how she was. Apparently she'd started feeling ill at school and they'd rung Vicky.' He paused to breathe. 'When I rang Vicky and asked her what the doctor had said she told me she hadn't been able to get an appointment so she'd just put Elizabeth to bed and let her sleep. At that point I knew. Don't ask me how, but I just knew it was serious. All I wanted to do was get home but the snow had made the roads almost impassable. Just like the other night.'

'It must have been terrible for you. I can imagine how helpless you must have felt.'

'I cannot tell you how bad that journey was, crawling through the snow, knowing that my daughter was sick. I rang Vicky again to tell her to take her to the Emergency Department but she told me I was overreacting and anyway she was just leaving for the party. We had a row. I told her she couldn't leave and she told me that if I'd been home on time it wouldn't have been an issue. She could have arrived at the party any time, but she wasn't going to let something as insignificant as a sick child ruin her social life.' The bitterness still flowed but it was weaker now, diluted by time. 'She left Elizabeth alone with an inexperienced babysitter. Call it instinct, but I called an ambulance and it arrived at the same time as I did. The moment I walked through the door I knew how sick she was. She was screaming. The screaming was terrible—' He stopped because thinking about it was just too painful. 'I saw that she had a rash. The paramedics were wonderful and they gave her antibiotics but it was too little too late. It was meningitis. The very worst type, with complications, and she went downhill so quickly it was shocking.'

'That's terrible. Truly awful.' Her arms tightened around him. 'But I don't see how, even in your darkest moments, you could blame yourself for any of that.'

'You want me to list the ways?' *There were so many.* 'If I hadn't gone to work that morning, if I'd chosen to take her to the doctor instead of leaving it to Vicky, if I'd left work earlier—she'd still be alive.'

'You don't know that.'

'But I don't *not* know it either, and living with that is hell.'

'When you left for work did you realise how ill she was?'

'Of course not. There were no signs she was ill at all.'

'Precisely. You didn't know. You had no way of knowing. Nor did you know that your wife wouldn't pay attention to the signs.'

'I should have known. She was always very clear about her priorities. Vicky never wanted Elizabeth any more than my mother had wanted me and she never made any secret of the fact that having a baby wasn't going to affect her life.' He turned his head to look at her, her features just visible in the semi-darkness. 'Now you're shocked.'

'Not shocked. Sad for Elizabeth. Sad for Vicky, I suppose, for never knowing how wonderful it is to love someone other than yourself.' She slid her hand over his chest. 'And sad for you, because you tried to be a family and it went badly wrong. But that wasn't your fault, Lucas.'

'I made her pregnant. That was my fault. I trusted her to show some responsibility towards our daughter that day and she didn't. I should have known she wouldn't. That was my fault too.'

'Your fault that another person put her own needs before that of a poorly child? I don't think so.'

'I knew what she was like.'

'You said you trusted her to show responsibility towards your daughter, which proves to me you still had faith in her. She let you down and that's terrible but it doesn't make it your fault.'

'Even if you're right, it doesn't make it better. My head is permanently filled with what-ifs. You name it, I thought it. I still think it. In the end none of it matters. All that matters is that I let my daughter down. I wasn't able to help her or protect her and she deserved so much better.'

'You're so wrong about that.' Her voice rang with sincerity, but her words of comfort slid off his skin like raindrops off a window, unable to penetrate the thick wall of guilt that had locked him in for years.

'I appreciate what you're trying to do, but you're the one who is wrong. You don't know what you're talking about.'

'Yes, I do. You're forgetting I saw the photograph. I saw a little girl with her arms around her daddy—a daddy she clearly adored. She didn't want or deserve better. She had everything she wanted and needed. You didn't let her down, Lucas.'

'If I'd been there she'd still be alive. Maybe I wasn't looking closely enough when we ate breakfast together. Maybe I missed something a better father would have noticed.'

'You were having breakfast with your daughter. I can tell you that from a child's point of view it doesn't get much better than that. You have to forgive yourself, Lucas. You have to accept that you did everything that could have been done. You have to accept that you were a good father but that even the best father can't protect a child from everything. Sometimes bad stuff happens and it's rubbish, but it's no one's fault and we have to stumble on the best we can until we start to function again.'

'I function. I've built a highly successful business.'

'But you don't have a family.'

'I don't want a family.' He'd made that decision in the weeks that had followed that terrible night. 'I tried. I failed. I don't want any of that. I certainly don't want the responsibility of a child.'

There was a long silence and then she pressed her lips to his shoulder. 'It must be terrifying, to have had that only to lose it. You *dare* not love because you loved so deeply and so fiercely and you lost.'

He grasped her hand and kissed her palm, breathing in the scent of her. 'I don't want to hurt you. I don't want you feeling anything for me.'

'What if it's too late? What if I tell you I already feel something?'

'I'd tell you it's the sex that makes you feel that way.'

'Really? I wouldn't know because it isn't something I do very often.'

'Which makes it even more likely that what

you're feeling is linked with the physical intimacy.'

'Or that what I feel is genuine. I have felt something for you for ages. Probably the reason I put up with your unreasonable demands in the office.' She took a deep breath and Lucas closed his eyes, willing her not to say what he guessed she was about to say.

'Emma, please don't—'

'Please don't say I love you? The trouble is, I do. I love you, Lucas.' She said it softly and then again, more firmly. 'I love you. And I'm not saying it because I want you to say it back or anything like that, but I want you to know how I feel. I know you don't like people saying it.'

So this was how it felt. 'No one has ever said it to me before.'

'What, *never*? What about Vicky?'

The mention of Vicky was enough to bring him to his senses. 'Vicky never loved me. She loved the idea of the two of us together. She loved the fact I had influential friends. And I didn't love her either.'

'Because you shut that side of yourself off when you were a child.' Her arms tightened around him. 'You are loved, Lucas, and you can love back.'

'Is that what you're waiting for? Because if so, you're wasting your time.' His voice rough, he cupped her face in his hands and looked down at her, refusing to be anything but honest. 'I can't say I love you. And I won't make you false promises. For me it's just sex and I'll move on because I always move on. It's the only way that works for me.' He was brutal because he had to be and he braced himself for her reaction. At the very least she'd walk away from him and sleep in the second bedroom.

But she did neither of those things.

Instead she kissed him again. 'Then we'd better make the most of tonight.'

Lucas was wide awake when he heard the knock on the door of the suite. He turned to look at Emma but she was still fast asleep so he rose quietly from the bed and pulled on a pair of jeans and a T-shirt before walking through the living room and opening the door.

It was Cristiano, and he was carrying his youngest daughter, Ella.

'Sorry to disturb you so early,' he said smoothly, 'but we have a family crisis. Our eldest, Chiara, has slipped and banged her head. Laurel and I are about to take her to hospital but we need some-one to watch Ella for a few hours.'

Lucas stared at his friend's child. Saw smiles and innocence. His pulse suddenly sprinted. 'The hotel has an excellent nanny service. I'll get you the number.'

'Laurel won't entertain leaving her with some-one we don't know. And neither would I.'

'Then ask a friend.'

'That's what I'm doing.' Cristiano's gaze didn't shift from his. 'I'm asking you.'

Lucas discovered that his mouth was so dry it was almost impossible to speak. 'You need to leave her with someone who can be trusted.'

'Which is why I knocked on your door, my friend.' Still holding his daughter, Cristiano put his hand on Lucas's shoulder. 'Laurel and I couldn't think of anyone we trust more than you. Will you take her? It will just be for a few hours.'

It was the ultimate vote of confidence but never had anyone's confidence seemed so mis-placed. He was the wrong person for this task.

Lucas looked at the little girl in his friend's arms, stared into dark curious eyes identical to Cristiano's. He knew her, of course, and she knew him. He'd been at her christening, at her first birthday party and endless other Ferrara events. He'd watched her grow from babe to toddler to little girl, but always from a safe distance and never from a position of responsibility.

'No. I can't—' But before the sentence was complete he found himself with his arms full of the little girl and she was so light, so fragile that he tightened his grip instantly in case he dropped her. Panic threatened to choke him because he knew with an absolute certainty that he couldn't do this. He didn't trust himself. His arms shook but the result of that weakness was that Ella simply wrapped her little arms around his neck, her soft curls brushing against his cheek.

'Fish! I want to see the fish—' She beamed past him towards the glass wall of the living room that formed a private aquarium, oblivious to the fact that right at that moment he was drowning in his own inadequacy.

Lucas was afraid to move in case he did something to damage this perfect human being, but she tugged at his shoulder insistently until he had no choice but to give in to her demands. Enchanted, she flattened her little hand on the glass, her fingers spread out like a starfish as she tried to 'touch' what she was seeing. So absorbed was she that she didn't even look round when her father spoke.

'*Grazie mille.* I will see you later and we're so grateful.'

Lucas turned his head, about to say that he couldn't do this, that he didn't *want* to do this, but Cristiano had already left and he was on his own with the child.

Emma stood in the bedroom, holding her breath as she listened through the door. She'd known the knock was coming and it had taken all her willpower to pretend to be asleep. Her feelings were a jumbled mess. The happiness and elation of their night together was mixed in with the utter misery of knowing that he didn't share her feelings. She knew she had a difficult decision facing her, but right now she concentrated on him. How would he cope?

She'd heard the agony in his voice as he'd spoken to his friend. She'd felt his pain and now she had a lump in her throat because she knew how hard this was for him. Her instinct was to rush out there and give him support, but Cristiano had made her promise not to do that because it would make it too easy for Lucas to hand over responsibility. They'd agreed that this strategy was worth a try so she stood still and listened as Ella chatted away to him, pointing out all the different fish. And she understood now what Cristiano had meant when he had told her quietly that if any child could give Lucas his confidence back it was little Ella. She was outgoing and confident, fascinated by the world around her and not at all shy or intimidated by Lucas. Another child might have been asking for her daddy, but not this one. In different circumstances Emma would have smiled because the little girl had so much of her father in her. No doubt she would one day be running the business Cristiano and his brother had turned into a global corporation, but for now she was taking charge of Lucas, telling him what she wanted to play with and exactly what he needed to do to make that happen.

'I brought my colouring pens. We can draw

the fish. And I want you to draw me a playhouse for my garden at home. Daddy says you draw buildings so you'd be the best person to do that.'

'I don't think—'

'I forgot to say please,' Ella muttered, contrite. 'Please. Please.'

'Well…all right. We'll design your playhouse together.'

'Can we have a fish tank in it? That way I can charge people to come and look at them.'

Emma smothered a smile, wondering if commercial vision was welded into the Ferrara DNA.

She wanted to see Lucas's expression but she didn't want to intrude on what was undoubtedly an important moment for him. The question was, would Ella's trust be enough to restore Lucas's belief in himself?

To prevent herself from walking out there to see what was happening, she went to the bathroom and locked herself in and spent the next hour relaxing in the bath, ready to leap out of the water if Lucas called.

But he didn't call. And when she'd dried her hair and dressed she just couldn't hide away any longer and walked into the living room to find both of them eating bowls of ice cream ordered from room service. Scattered on the floor next to them were several large pieces of paper covered in pencil drawings.

Emma raised her eyebrows. 'This looks fun.'

'We're playing tea parties. Lucas let me order from room service.' Ella pushed a spoon towards her doll as she pretended to 'feed' her. 'Guess what? Lucas has designed me a playhouse. I helped.'

Lucas, Lucas, Lucas. Every other word was Lucas.

Emma knelt down on the floor next to the little girl and looked more closely at the drawings. Like most architects, Lucas usually used computer software for his plans. In this case he'd used a ruler and pencil but the drawing was no less detailed for the lack of technology or the unusual nature of the 'building'. Emma caught his eye and he gave a faint smile as he read her mind.

'North elevation,' he said quietly. 'I didn't see any reason not to do it properly. It's a relief to know I can still use a pencil.'

A lump grew in her throat. This was a man

who had designed some of the most iconic structures of recent years and there was something endearing about the attention he'd given to this project. Just one glance told her that Ella Ferrara was going to have the most beautiful playhouse any child had ever had.

Ella finished her ice cream and sprawled on her stomach, absorbed by the project they were creating together, oblivious to the significance of the encounter. 'Can I colour it in?'

'Colour away.' Lucas handed her the coloured pens and she took them and stared hard at the drawing.

'Lucas, can it have a chimney?'

He studied the drawing. 'Now why didn't I think of that? A chimney would be perfect. Where do you think it should go?'

'Here.' She stabbed her finger into the paper and Lucas handed her the pencil.

'Good decision. Draw it on. And any time you want to join my company just let me know.'

'You two have certainly been busy.' Smiling, Emma sat down next to them and helped herself to ice cream. 'Healthy breakfast, Lucas.'

'One bowl of ice cream isn't going to hurt her.

We've ordered toast if you'd rather wait for that. You might want to move that chimney to the right a bit, Ella—'

Watching the little girl carefully drawing a chimney onto the plans while Lucas helped her, Emma wondered if he even realised how natural he was with the child and how much time had passed while the two of them had been designing their playhouse. At some point over the last few hours he'd forgotten the weight of responsibility and focused instead on just occupying her. And whatever he believed about himself, Emma saw the care he showed. It was evident in everything. From his infinite patience with the little girl, to the way he listened carefully to her every request.

When room service arrived with an order of hot toast, it was Lucas who spread the butter and then deftly cut windows and a door before presenting it to the little girl.

Watching, Emma wondered if he even realised what he'd just done.

'Oh!' Ella's face brightened as she stared at the plate. 'A toast house. With a chimney. I want my toast like this always and for ever. You have to teach my dad.'

Lucas stared at the plate, his breathing shallow.

Staring at the intimidating set of his features, Ella's smile faltered. 'I forgot the please again,' she said in a small voice. 'You're angry because I forgot the please.'

He squatted down to her level and smiled at her. 'I'm not angry. And I'm glad you like the toast.'

'It's the best thing ever.' Ella hesitated and then reached out and picked up the chimney. 'I'm eating the chimney first. Then I'm going to eat the door.'

Over the top of her head, Lucas's eyes met Emma's briefly and then he turned his attention back to the child. 'Ella, this is my friend Emma and you're going to play with her for a while because I have to—'

'You can't leave.' Ella slipped her hand into his. 'Our house isn't finished. If you're hungry, you can share my toast.' Carefully, she selected a window and slid it into Lucas's mouth.

'Ella—'

'More?'

'No.' His voice was hoarse. 'No more.'

'You forgot to say thank you.' Ella gave him a sympathetic look. 'Don't worry. Remembering is hard, isn't it?'

Lucas breathed deeply. 'Yes. Remembering is hard.'

'I'll help you if you help me.' Ella crawled onto his lap with the rest of her toast. 'I like staying with you. It's fun and you don't tell me off when I forget to say please. Can we do this again?'

Emma discovered that she was holding her breath. Perhaps it was too much. Perhaps it just wasn't going to—

'Yes—' Lucas rescued the plate before the buttered toast landed on his lap '—we can do this again. I'm going to be coming to Sicily soon to discuss a new hotel with your daddy. If you like, I could build that playhouse for you.'

'Perfect.' Ella beamed and flung her arms around his neck and Emma turned away quickly, tidying up some crayons to hide the tears on her face.

He'd made her a toast house, the way he used to with his daughter. And now he was promising to help her build the playhouse. That was progress, surely?

It was too soon to be sure, but she was confident that Cristiano's idea had been a good one. He'd trusted his friend with his most precious possession and that trust would hopefully propel Lucas forward a few steps.

And she had to move forward too. She had to stop avoiding things that she found difficult and face them.

She had to have an honest conversation with her sister.

Knowing that it was time to leave, she made her excuses and left the two of them together while she returned to her own bedroom to pack, breaking off only to send an email.

'This came for you.' Lucas stood in the doorway, an envelope in his hand and his eyes on the suitcase. 'You're still planning on leaving today?'

'I want to spend time with Jamie. Has Ella gone?'

'Cristiano just picked her up.' His eyes were still on the suitcase. 'Apparently Chiara is doing fine.'

Emma kept her eyes down, afraid of revealing that there had never been anything wrong with the eldest Ferrara daughter. They'd all agreed that only the threat of an emergency would have induced Lucas to look after the little girl and it had been worth the deception.

His hand covered hers as she pushed a pair of shoes into the case. 'If I asked you to stay another day, would you?' His tone was raw and her heart pounded.

'Is some aspect of my work unfinished?'

'This isn't about work. The work is done. If you stayed it would be about the two of us.'

Emma closed her eyes because it was so, so tempting. It would have been so easy to stay. So easy to fool herself that if she stayed his feelings might change. But she wasn't going to do that to herself. Or to him.

Reluctantly, she extracted her hand from his, horrified by how difficult it felt to do that. 'I have to go, Lucas.'

'One more day.'

'I can't.'

There was a long, tense silence and then he stepped back, his eyes guarded. 'Right. Good decision. I'll see you back in the office after Christmas. Aren't you going to open the letter?'

'It's not for me.' She folded the last of her clothes into the case she'd bought at the mall. 'It's for you. You should open it. It will save me the bother of putting it in another envelope.' From behind her she could hear the sound of the envelope being torn open. And then there was silence.

'Your letter of resignation.' His voice was flat and devoid of expression. 'I thought we'd dealt with this once. You agreed there was no need for you to leave.'

'There was no need to leave when we'd had one night of sex.' Emma closed the case and lifted it off the bed and onto the floor. 'There is every reason to leave now I know I'm in love with you.'

He stilled. 'About that—'

'If you're going to tell me that I don't know my own mind, then let me stop you right there.' She let go of the case and straightened. 'I've told you about my father, but I've never told you about my mother.'

'Your mother?'

'She had a real talent for falling in love with men who couldn't love her back. Instead of walking away, somehow she always managed to convince herself that if she stuck at it, they'd come round. She did it with my father, even after he walked out leaving her to cope with a baby on her own. And then she did the same thing with her boss.' She saw understanding dawn in his eyes and nodded. 'That's right. Jamie is the result of an affair that my mother had with her boss. She fell in love with him. Unfortunately he didn't feel the same way about her but instead of leaving, she stayed. And the longer she stayed, the more she hoped.' And, for the first time, she'd been given a glimpse of just how hard it had probably been for her mother. And how easy it would be to take strands of hope and spin them into something substantial and meaningful.

'Emma—'

'No, don't say a word. You have no idea how much I want to pretend to myself that I can carry on working for you and that the way I feel won't be a problem. But I know it will be a problem. I'll have to see you every day, but not tell you how I feel. I'll have to take phone calls from the women you see and keep smiling while I do it, and I can't do that, Lucas.' She had to force the words out. 'I won't live my life hoping that one day I'm going to wake up and find my dream has become reality. I won't do that to myself.'

He watched her for a long moment and then paced across the elegant bedroom and stared out across the private swimming pool.

She waited for him to say what he was thinking and, as the silence stretched, so a tiny flicker of hope bloomed somewhere deep inside her. Even without her permission, it bloomed. And this was how it started, she thought. If she stayed, it would be like this. In every word and action, she'd be searching for a different meaning. Hoping, just as she was hoping now.

He drew back his shoulders, those strong, muscular shoulders that she now knew so well.

'You have a notice period.' His voice was businesslike. 'It won't be easy to replace you.'

And, just like that, hope died. The pain was sharp, like falling onto broken glass. She wondered if her mother had felt like that every day and, if so, how she had managed to get back up and keep going back for more.

'There's no need to worry about replacing me. I've already done it. Fiona Hawkings is currently working for John in Accounts and she's just what you need. Efficient, competent and not remotely interested in anything except a professional relationship. She was going to cover for me during my holiday so she's already fully briefed and if she has a problem then she has my number.'

Lucas's expression didn't change. 'You already had someone lined up?'

'If I'd been knocked over by a bus, someone needed to know how to run your office. So you're sorted. No need to worry.'

'And what about you? Is it wise to give up your job without another one to go to?'

No. But it was wiser than staying because every day she stayed would make it harder to leave. 'I'll be fine. I'm good at what I do. I'm going to find a job nearer to home and try and get some sort of balance in my life. I certainly don't have that at the moment. I want to spend time with Jamie, not just at weekends, but during the week too. I want to be able to go out in

he evening occasionally without feeling guilty
because I'm only at home for forty-eight hours.'
She gave a half smile. 'I want to go dancing.'
She said the words even though right now she
didn't feel as if she'd ever be able to dance again.

'Will your sister approve?'

'Probably not.' And telling her was something
she was dreading. 'That's something I need to
deal with, I know I do. I've been avoiding it because it felt difficult.'

'Talking of avoiding things because they feel
difficult—' his voice was harsh '—was it your
idea to give Ella to me to look after?'

She shook her head. 'Cristiano's. You think
you've never been loved, Lucas, but you're so
wrong. Maybe your family didn't love you but
you have friends who love you. Cristiano and
Laurel, Mal—' she blushed '—I mean the Crown
Prince. They all love you like a brother. And
Ella, of course—' she managed a light smile
—she adores you.'

His gaze didn't shift from her face. 'And you.'

'Yes, me. But I don't love you as a brother.'
Trying not to think about that, she picked up her

case. 'I'm not using the jet. I'm not working for you any more so it seemed like a liberty.'

'For heaven's sake, Emma, use the jet.' He sounded irritable and angry but she knew it was just because she'd shaken up his routine. Lucas Jackson liked his life to run smoothly and her leaving was threatening that. He was worried that his business would suffer.

'Goodbye Lucas. Be kind to Fiona. And to yourself.' And without looking back, she walked towards the door.

'I'll hold the job open until the end of the month. Just in case your sister has a meltdown.'

'You don't need to do that. When I explain, she'll understand.'

CHAPTER NINE

'YOU resigned? Oh my God, are you *mad*?'

'I'm not mad. It was a well thought out decision.' The only decision she could have made and she clung to that belief as her sister's censorship and judgement eroded her self-confidence like acid rain. 'Don't worry, Angie. I'll find another job. And please calm down or you'll worry Jamie.'

'Worry Jamie? What about me? Don't you think I'm worried? I don't earn enough to support us all, Emma. I already have enough responsibility.'

'I don't expect you to support us all and I intend to take on more of the responsibility.' Emma forced herself to stay calm. 'I've told you—I'll find another job. I've already started to look and I've called a few people I know.'

'Why didn't you do that before you resigned? I mean why the sudden hurry? What happened?'

Her sister paced the tiny kitchen and then suddenly stopped and turned, eyes riveted to Emma's face. 'Oh no—' Her voice dropped to a whisper. 'You slept with him, didn't you? You slept with your boss. *That's* what happened.'

Hearing her sister reduce her feelings to no more than a sordid encounter upset her more than she would have imagined possible. Suddenly she wished she had a different relationship with her sister. One in which she could confide and express her real feelings. She thought about the lovely chat she'd had with Avery and wished it could have been that way with her sister. The irony was that she'd been more open and honest with Lucas than she was with Angie. 'I'll get another job. That's all you need to know.'

Angie didn't appear to be listening. 'Knowing what happened to Mum, you slept with your boss?'

'I am *not* Mum. This is different.'

'How is it different?' Angie started clattering around the kitchen, crashing mugs together as she unloaded the dishwasher. 'Don't tell me, you love him and you think if you resign you can have a relationship. You think he'll suddenly waltz up here and ask you to marry him, is that it? Oh God, you're *exactly* like her. Delusional! A total dreamer.'

Emma was shaking. 'I am none of those things and that isn't what I'm thinking. I'm *nothing* like Mum and I don't want to talk about it any more because you just don't listen.' She couldn't even allow herself to think how her life was going to be without Lucas. It had only been a day and already she was aching.

But her sister seemed oblivious to her feelings. 'You had an amazing job and you've thrown it all away for nothing.' Another clatter of plates. 'You seem to have forgotten your responsibility towards Jamie. Lucas Jackson is not the settling-down type, Emma. Anyone can see that.'

'And I don't blame him for that, given his experience of family.' Struggling with her own feelings, unable to cope with her sister's too, Emma lost it. 'And you are supposed to be *my* family. You are supposed to love me and care about me. Instead all you do is yell at me and blame me and think about yourself.'

Angie looked taken aback. 'I do love you! That's why I'm so upset that you've done this.'

'No. You're upset that I've "done this" because you're worried about the impact it's going to have on *your* life.' Emma wrapped her arms around herself. 'You don't care about my life. You don't care that I'm in love with Lucas or that I'm hurting or that the thought of a life without him is breaking my heart. You don't care about any of that.'

'You're in love with him? You really are?' Angie looked so appalled that Emma closed her eyes.

'Yes, but if you're worried I'm going to be like Mum then don't be. I know he doesn't love me back so I'm not going to be hanging around waiting for that to happen. He can't love because he's hurting so badly—'

Angie looked baffled. 'How is *he* hurting?'

'Never mind. It doesn't matter. I shouldn't have said anything—' Her voice broke and she turned away but the next moment Angie had dumped the plates and suddenly she had her arms around Emma and they were hugging in a way they'd never hugged before.

'I'm sorry. I didn't know you were in love with him. I would have done anything for that not to happen. I saw how badly that affected Mum.'

Angie was crying too and hugging her so tightly that Emma could hardly breathe. 'I'm sorry you're so hurt. I *do* care. You have no idea. It's just that I promised Mum I'd look after you and Jamie and not let anything happen to you and I feel like I've failed because you've gone and done *exactly* what she did. I never, ever wanted you to be hurt in this way. I did everything I could to protect you from it.'

'This is life, Angie, and you can't stop life happening. And you haven't failed. You held it all together and you gave up so much so that we could be a family, I'm not surprised you feel resentful about that sometimes. You wouldn't be human if you didn't.' Sniffing, Emma pulled away even though it felt surprisingly good to be held. 'But that is going to change. I'm going to find a job closer to home so that I can take care of Jamie and you can go to college.'

'I couldn't do that.'

'Why not?'

'Because I'm the head of the family.'

Emma shook her head, realising for the first time just how much responsibility their mother had loaded onto her elder sister. 'No. You've allowed me to do a job I love. Now it's your turn. Life doesn't have to be a self-sacrifice, Angie. Maybe it isn't possible to have it all, but we can do better than this.'

Jamie came running into the room and stopped dead when he saw them, the excitement in his face replaced by anxiety. 'What's the matter? What's wrong? Why are you both crying?'

'Nothing.' Angie pulled away, smiling. 'We're just hugging. Sisters hug. Anything wrong with that?'

'No.' Jamie looked at them curiously and Emma wrapped him in her arms, grateful for her family and trying to ignore the horrible, hollow ache in her gut.

'It's so good to be home. I missed you.' Determined not to mope, she released him. She had to pull herself together because the last thing she wanted was for Jamie to guess how bad she was feeling. 'Sorry it took me so long to get here.'

'It doesn't matter. I was at Sam's and that was really cool because he has a new puppy. And I played with the Lego Lucas sent. I can't wait to show you.'

Frowning, Emma released him. 'Lego?'

'The Star Wars ship. It arrived the day you flew to...to...that place.'

'Zubran. Lucas sent you Lego? But how did he even know it's your favourite?' And then she remembered that she'd mentioned it. Just once. The morning after they'd— She swallowed. 'Was there a note with it?'

Jamie poured cereal into a bowl, oblivious of the significance of the gift. 'Yes, but it was short. It just said he was sorry he had to borrow you or something and that the Lego would keep me busy until you came home. Can I have sugar on my cereal?'

'No.' Both girls spoke simultaneously and Emma felt her heart pound.

'That was a thoughtful, generous thing to do.'

Angie shot her a warning look. 'And that's all it was. A thoughtful and generous gesture. And quite right too. Don't go getting any ideas. Don't read anything into it. You are *not* going down that route. Remember?'

But over the next few days, Emma discovered just how hard it was to kill hope. Every time the

phone rang, her heart jumped. Every time someone knocked on the door, she held her breath.
But it was never Lucas and the disappointment
was like a physical blow. The effort of keeping
a smile on her face exhausted her. Inside she felt
hollow and miserable and it must have showed
because Angie started to fuss over her in a way
she'd never fussed before. Or maybe it was just
that their relationship had changed. Certainly
they were talking more and Emma had even persuaded her sister to pick up a prospectus from
the local college.

Two days later she had a call from Cristiano
Ferrara, offering her a job.

'I heard that you resigned,' he said, his Sicilian
accent more pronounced over the phone, 'and I
didn't want you to be snapped up by anyone else.
You can work from home or we'll find you an
office, whichever you prefer. I don't care where
you are as long as you work for me. Our business is growing and it would be useful to have
someone based in the UK.'

Emma listened as he outlined terms that were
ridiculously generous and all the time he was
speaking she just wanted to ask about Lucas.

She wanted to know if he was all right. If he was working too hard. If he'd changed since he'd looked after little Ella.

But she didn't, because she knew she had no right to know the answer to any of those questions.

And she accepted the job without hesitation, ignoring that tiny part of her that said she was only doing it because it meant retaining a tiny link with Lucas. That wasn't it. What person in their right mind would turn down the chance to work for the Ferrara Group? Especially at the terms he was offering.

They agreed to sort out details in the New Year and Emma came off the phone wondering why she couldn't feel more elated.

Angie squealed with excitement when she told her and Jamie was delighted that she wasn't going to be away so much.

Emma couldn't even bring herself to think about working for someone who wasn't Lucas.

A few days after the madness of Christmas, she was standing in Jamie's bedroom, staring at the

Star Wars Lego and wondering again why Lucas had sent it, when the doorbell rang.

Jamie and Emma had gone to scour the sales for bargains and she was alone in the house so she had no choice but to answer the door herself.

Lucas stood there holding a handful of crumpled papers, his Lamborghini attracting a crowd of awed teenagers in the street outside. 'Can I come in?'

Emma looked at him stupidly, resisting the temptation to fling herself at him like a puppy greeting its owner. *So* handsome, she thought, as she looked at that dark hair brushing the collar of the black cashmere coat. Handsome and guarded. 'I thought you were in Zubran.'

'Not any more. Are you going to let me in or slam the door in my face?'

Her heart skidded in her chest. She told herself firmly that what he was going to say wasn't going to be what she wanted him to say. It would be something to do with work. Something she'd forgotten to hand over to Fiona. 'You can come in, but I can't vouch for the safety of your car if you leave it there.'

'I don't care about my car.' Without waiting

for her to move aside, he stepped past her and the brush of his body against hers caused them both to tense.

They created it between them, she thought. The electricity.

His eyes narrowed. 'You've lost weight.'

Emma thought of Avery and lifted her chin. *Pride.* No way was she going to let him know how bad she felt. 'No, I haven't,' she lied, 'it's just what I'm wearing. What's that in your hand? If it's a contract, forget it. I'm already working for someone else.'

'I know. Cristiano. Good. I'm glad that's sorted out.'

Emma closed the front door, thinking that the narrow hallway of their home wasn't the best place to be trapped with a man of his physique. She wanted to keep her distance, but there wasn't enough room to keep her distance when he dominated the limited space. 'You told him to employ me?'

'I can't tell Cristiano Ferrara who to employ. I merely told him you were available. He's a bright guy. I knew it would be a matter of hours before he offered you a job.' There was something different about him. Something in his eyes. A new energy and she felt relieved to see it because she'd been so worried about him.

'You're not here to ask me to work for you again?'

'No. I don't want you working for me again. Fiona is working out nicely. You were right about her. She's great.'

'Oh. Right. Well, that's—' her ego absorbed the blow '—good. That's really good.'

'Yes, it is good, because you have this thing about not having a relationship with your boss,' he said softly, 'so I don't want to be your boss any more.'

Emma felt strangely dizzy.

She was doing it again, she thought. Imagining things she shouldn't be imagining. Dreaming dreams she shouldn't be dreaming.

'Why don't you want to be my boss any more?'

'You're a bright girl. I would have thought it was obvious.'

Emma lifted her hand to her throat, too scared to speak.

He raised an eyebrow. 'Aren't you going to say something?' The corners of his mouth—

'at beautiful sexy mouth—flickered. 'I've never
nown you short of words before.'

'If you don't want me to work for you then…
hose papers in your hand aren't a contract?'

'No.' He handed them to her and she smoothed
hem with shaking hands and saw that she was
olding a picture of a house, obviously drawn
y a child but surprisingly detailed.

'Oh. Did Ella do this?'

'No. I did it.' His voice was rough. 'I was six
ears old and living in one small room with a
voman who didn't want me.'

Emma looked at him, the breath jammed in
er throat. His mother. He was talking about his
nother. 'You drew it?'

'Living in that small room with just one tiny
vindow felt wrong to me. To block it out I
lreamed of the house I wanted to live in. I prom-
sed myself that one day I'd build it and to make
ure I never forgot, I drew it. You're holding that
lrawing.'

'You kept it.'

'Yes. Because I never wanted to forget where
I came from.'

The lump stung her throat as she thought of

the little boy dreaming of his escape. 'Why are you showing me this?'

'Because it's time to build that house. I've built structures for many people, but never a home for myself because home meant family and I've always shied away from that for all the reasons you already know. Even when I married Vicky I didn't build this home. She chose an expensive house in an expensive road and I paid for it. But now I'm ready to build something special. And what I want to know is—' he hesitated, his gaze fixed on her face '—will you live in it with me?'

The papers slid from her fingers onto the floor. 'Me?'

'Yes, because a house is just a building. It's the people in it that make it a home and that's what I want. A proper home.' Stooping, he recovered the drawings. 'It doesn't have to be exactly like this. You can help me improve it. And Jamie had better have some input as he'll be living in it too. And I thought we could build a separate house for your sister in the grounds, so that she can have her own life but still be part of ours if she wants that.'

'Part of ours?' If she'd been scared before, she

was terrified now. Terrified that what she was imagining wasn't what he was asking. That his intentions might not match her hopes. That she might fall as her mother had fallen, and then tumble to her feet only to fall again. 'I don't understand what you're asking. I don't understand what you're telling me.'

He put the drawings on the hall table. 'I'm asking you to marry me. I'm asking you to live with me so that we can be a family. I'm telling you that I love you.'

Emma closed her eyes, unable to believe what he was saying. 'You can't love. It's the one thing you can't do. You don't *want* to do it.'

'I've discovered I was wrong about that. Apparently I can love.' He cupped her face in his hands and lowered his mouth to hers, kissing her gently. 'I love *you*. And I want to be with you, always. I can build you a house, Emma, I'm good at that part. But you have to help me make it a home. That's the bit I'm no good at. But you are. I've never met anyone like you before. You're fiercely loyal and determined. That night in the snow—I sent you away, but you wouldn't leave.'

'How could I leave you? I was so worried about you.'

'I was unforgivably rude to you.'

'Not rude. Just hurting.' She touched his face with her fingers, still unable to believe that he'd actually said he loved her. 'I stayed because I wanted to.'

'And last year—' he breathed deeply '—you stayed then too.'

'I only put a blanket over you, I didn't know what else to do.'

'And you locked the door and made sure no one saw me like that. And then brought me strong coffee all morning and fielded my calls, without ever putting pressure on me to tell you what was wrong.'

'I suppose I knew you wouldn't want to talk about it. And now I know, I'm not surprised you were drunk—' she slid her arms around his waist '—you suffered a terrible loss.'

'Yes. And that doesn't go away,' he said quietly, 'but spending time with you made me look at it differently. And look at myself differently. And then you and Cristiano cooked up that plan for me to have Ella.'

'It was Cristiano's idea. I was worried it might have been too much but he was determined to do something. He just made me promise not to come out of the bedroom and take over.'

His eyes gleamed. 'So you left me to struggle.'

'No, I left you to cope. And I hoped that once you realised you were coping, you'd start to regain your confidence. And you did.'

'Yes,' he said slowly, 'I did.'

'You've never even told me what happened to Vicky. Were you divorced?'

'We were never married. The moment I found out she was pregnant, I wanted her to marry me, but she wouldn't make that commitment. She thought it would make her less marketable. She didn't want to be seen as a "mother". The only thing that was keeping us together was Elizabeth and after she died, we went our separate ways. Last thing I heard Vicky was in Australia but we don't keep in touch.'

'I'm sorry.'

'Don't be. It was never a relationship. That was the problem. And I told myself I didn't want to even try it again. That night in the castle—it was so hard to tell you I wanted to keep it professional.' He lowered his mouth to hers and kissed her slowly and deliberately, until she gave a low moan and pressed against him.

'I really believed that was what you wanted. Then I started to wonder. Your reaction over the red dress—I thought you were just angry but Avery thought it was something different.'

He smiled against her lips. 'Avery is too astute for her own good.'

'I like her *so* much. She was the one who persuaded me to just dress up and have a good time. So that's what I did. I really didn't think anything would happen. And then you were so angry that I danced with Carlo—'

'Jealous—' Lucas groaned '—and *not* proud of it. But it was seeing you with him that made me realise that I didn't want to keep things professional. I'd never felt that way before.'

'I hadn't either. I'd always promised myself that I'd never fall for my boss and I really tried to stick to that, but I decided that night that I just wanted to spend whatever time I could with you. That I'd rather find another job if I had to.'

'I can't believe you sacrificed so much to support your family.' He gathered her close. 'When

I think of the number of times I kept you working late at the office, not knowing that you were going home alone to a rented room.'

'I liked working late. Probably because I loved being with you.'

'I was a nightmare boss.'

'No! That isn't true. You were an excellent boss.'

'You slog your guts out during the week to earn money for your family and then you rush back here at weekends so that you can take care of them, not because you have to but because you want to. I've never seen that commitment in anyone. To be honest I didn't even believe it existed. You're so special.'

'I'm not special,' she stammered, 'I'm boringly ordinary. There are loads of people like me around.'

'Not true. And anyway, the only person I'm interested in is you. And because I'm horribly selfish I want you all to myself. I want you with a piece of paper binding you to me and I want you wearing my ring on your finger so that if I drive you mad you won't walk out.'

'I'd never walk out!' Emma was shocked that

he'd even suggest it and then remembered that he'd never had any stability in his life, ever, and that realisation made her hug him all the more tightly because she was determined to change all that. 'You're so incredibly talented and clever and you've built so many things, but you've never had foundations of your own. You don't have to worry about me leaving. I'd never leave. I love you so much.'

'I know. And I'm so lucky that you love me. You are the most loyal, loving person I've ever met.' He buried his fingers in her hair and kissed her again. 'You've stuck with your sister and brother, no matter what. You took a job that paid well so that you could support them even though it meant living away from them. I've never met anyone as unselfish as you.'

'I wasn't that unselfish,' Emma murmured, leaning her head against his chest. 'I loved my job. Or at least, I loved being with you every day. Seeing you. I've missed you so badly it's been agony although very good for the figure.'

'You can still be with me every day, only you won't be working with me.' He stroked her hair. 'You haven't answered my question.'

'Question?'

'I asked you to marry me. It would be nice to have an answer.'

Emma felt as if she were walking on air. 'I thought the answer was obvious. I've already told you I love you. The answer is yes, of course. A huge yes. A massive yes.'

He slid his hand into his pocket and pulled out a box. Flipping open the lid, he removed a flawless diamond ring. 'Just so that you can't change your mind, I bought you this.'

Emma gaped. 'It's…huge.'

'I want other men to be able to see from a distance that you're mine.'

She gave a choked laugh as he slid it onto her finger. 'They can probably see it from Zubran. It's—' she felt overwhelmed, not just by the ring but by the sentiment behind it '—it's beautiful, Lucas but I think I'm too scared to wear anything this valuable. I'll need a bodyguard.'

'You have me.' Lucas lifted her hand to his lips and kissed it. 'And I'm going to build you a house that will keep you and the ring safe, but in the meantime how would you feel about taking the whole family to Sicily for a holiday?'

'Sicily?'

'I owe a certain little girl a playhouse. It's a small price to pay for what she did for me,' he said in a husky voice and Emma blinked back the tears that clouded her vision.

'I think a holiday in Sicily sounds perfect.'×

* * * * *

Mills & Boon® Large Print
March 2013

A NIGHT OF NO RETURN
Sarah Morgan

A TEMPESTUOUS TEMPTATION
Cathy Williams

BACK IN THE HEADLINES
Sharon Kendrick

A TASTE OF THE UNTAMED
Susan Stephens

THE COUNT'S CHRISTMAS BABY
Rebecca Winters

HIS LARKVILLE CINDERELLA
Melissa McClone

THE NANNY WHO SAVED CHRISTMAS
Michelle Douglas

SNOWED IN AT THE RANCH
Cara Colter

EXQUISITE REVENGE
Abby Green

BENEATH THE VEIL OF PARADISE
Kate Hewitt

SURRENDERING ALL BUT HER HEART
Melanie Milburne

LP

Mills & Boon® Large Print
April 2013

A RING TO SECURE HIS HEIR
Lynne Graham

WHAT HIS MONEY CAN'T HIDE
Maggie Cox

WOMAN IN A SHEIKH'S WORLD
Sarah Morgan

AT DANTE'S SERVICE
Chantelle Shaw

THE ENGLISH LORD'S SECRET SON
Margaret Way

THE SECRET THAT CHANGED EVERYTHING
Lucy Gordon

THE CATTLEMAN'S SPECIAL DELIVERY
Barbara Hannay

HER MAN IN MANHATTAN
Trish Wylie

AT HIS MAJESTY'S REQUEST
Maisey Yates

BREAKING THE GREEK'S RULES
Anne McAllister

THE RUTHLESS CALEB WILDE
Sandra Marton

APL		CCS	
Cen		Ear	
Mob		Cou	
ALL		Jub	
WH		CHE	
Aid		Bel	
Fin		Fol	
Can		STO	
Til		HCL	